I0622013

A Hind Let Loose by C. E. Montague

Charles Edward Montague was born in London on New Year's Day, 1867 and educated at the City of London School and then Balliol College, Oxford.

At university, Montague, a keen writer, wrote several literary reviews for the Manchester Guardian and was then invited for a month's trial and, after impressing, to work there.

Montague and the editor, C. P. Scott shared the same political views and between them they turned the Manchester Guardian into a vibrant and campaigning newspaper. They were for Irish Home Rule and against the Boer War and the First World War.

But now that the war had begun. Montague believed that it was important to give full and unequivocal support to the British government. Despite his age, 47, he was determined to serve.

Montague was soon promoted to the rank of second lieutenant and with it a transfer to Military Intelligence. The war also brought about a crisis in his faith and it was resolved by Montague temporarily putting it to one side and carrying on with the fighting.

In November 1918 the war was over and Montague could now return home to his wife and family and also to the Manchester Guardian where he would continue to work until retirement in 1925.

For Montague the war had been corrosive but it had given him much to write about both for the paper but also for his books which he now hoped to also spend more time on. Among those to flow from his pen are the novels A Hind Let Loose and Rough Justice as well as collections of short stories, other essays and a travel book.

He finally retired in 1925, and settled down to become a full-time writer in the last years of his life. Charles Edward Montague died in Manchester on May 28th, 1928 at the age of 61.

Index of Contents

CHAPTER I

They grew in beauty, side by side;
They filled one home with glee.
F. TIEMANS

Halland, like some others, is the second city of the Empire. Halland admits it; you don't, she says, get over figures; and yet she cannot help knowing how London might have flagged, long ago, without all the new Halland blood in its veins—let in pretty often by poor, soft lads who never could have kept their feet in the rush of life and work in the stern North—just men enough to work the milder scrummage of the capital.

An immemorial self-respect has handed down to the Halland of to-day the pick of a dozen warming aphorisms. The best known, perhaps, is: "England is Halland and water; Halland is England neat." "What Halland thinks to-day, England will think to-morrow," dates, it is thought, from the first Halland man. "Take away Halland and twelve miles round, and where are you?" is dearer to the suburbs. And the great love she bears herself is no mere doting on her beauty; it kisses each mole. Well enough in your garden South, where work is play, to fuss about clean rivers. Leal Halland men, homing from Florence, San Francisco, or Constantinople, will pause entranced, on leaving the station, to lean over the Prince Consort Bridge—already an antique, only a smoke-cured one it is true, but senior in looks to Trojan's Arch at Ancona—and come into their own again. Below, on the torpid stream, refuse oils draw sheeny curvilinear grainings, parodies of a rainbow's palette, on a chocolate ground; late at night the quiet lifts into relief the still, small, multitudinous plop of bubbles rising and breaking, a million infinitesimal belches. Day or night, as at the passing of Cleopatra's barge,

A faint, invisible perfume hits the sense
Of the adjacent wharves,

wharves partly, factories mostly, springing their sixty feet of sheer out of the viscous fluid, their walls bored here and there with pipes of all calibres, some spitting fitful white rods of steam; from others, their nozzles flush with the bricks, all the waste filths of industry, bilges and rinsings' and dirt-gorged greases, suppurate slowly and cake on the walls, coat upon coat. You might say, not having love, "A Venice in Hell"; but what are Thames and Tiber, Abana and Pharpar, to this Jordan, for this Israel? What are outlandish fads of manner, either? Nasty fops' tricks, taints that the best of us may pick up more or less in the alien's trains and tables d'hote. But the leprous scales fall from the exiles, back in the old place. *Largior hos aether campos.* Here they feel clean and blunt again; "jannock" they call it; the dialect word enshrines Halland's faith that to be a diamond you must be rough.

No two stouter pillars of this faith, no more affluent springs of corresponding works than the two Halland daily papers: the Warder, Conservative; the Stalwart, Liberal; each owned and ruled and, as any

Halland man could tell you, written, for these eighty years past, by its own dynasty of editors, born and trained for their high duties, each of them

. . . the destined heir,
From his soft cradle, of his father's chair.

For eighty years a reigning Brumby and a reigning Pinn had stoked the city's passion for calling spades, at the very least, spades. Unthinking people call animosities sterile. This one, of Brumby and Pinn, made Halland's world go round as surely as, by flying at each other's heads, your positive and negative electric currents turn the wheels of Halland's tram-cars.

Not that the Warder and Stalwart could never agree. There is a time, both knew, to embrace, as well as a time, a larger time, to refrain from embracing. Let a stranger give the name of goose to the least among the local swans and he will see. That critical time when the statue of Binney, the Halland philanthropist, had to be ordered, when the claims of Tom Bumup, a local man, a man genuinely self-taught, who had learnt his art, absolutely without exception, in our city, and no mere sculptor either but a man of sterling worth, jannock, if ever man was, and a man with many mouths at home to feed—when Tom's claim, or rather his right, to the job was questioned by a set of faddists, friends of every city, every country but their own, who would, if they could, have given the work to one Alfred Gilbert (some pushing London man), or even to a foreigner, called, I think, Rodin—then, I say, begging your pardon for thus gasping, but such disloyal conduct makes one breathless, just to write of it—then, I say, the two gallant enemies, terrible as the sea but also as sane as it, dropped their points, stood by their menaced fellow-citizen until his peril was past, and enriched their city for all time with the most faithful marble image, I do believe, in all Western Europe, of a snow man touched with a spiritual fineness by the first hour of a thaw.

Both dynasties, indeed, were friend to the arts. When old George Brumby's death "severed," as even the Stalwart admitted, "one of the few remaining links with the past," he left by his will to the Halland College of Music, £4,000, a good half of the gleanings of the thrift that for so many years had had the city's music noticed in the Warder by any young reporter not yet up, for want of shorthand, to serious things. It was letters, rather, that Pinn cherished in his bosom—Elijah Pinn, now on the throne. When he ascended, twenty-six years ago, he found that, absorbed in the strenuous parts of life, the Stalwart had left unobserved the issue of the works of Ruskin, Carlyle, Tennyson, Browning, and George Eliot, in which, as he shrewdly said in the idiom of his calling, considerable and increasing sections of the public were unquestionably interested. Acting on this piece of insight, he beat up some twenty to thirty widows and daughters of Nonconformist ministers of the best type, widows and virgins whose cruses and lamps were not too full of oil for his purpose; and to these he gave out for review the new novels, histories, epics, philosophies, systems of medicine, astronomy, jurisprudence, tactics, and the rest. True, the ladies were not all pundits; but Pinn, for whom no trouble was too great, taught them critical method, arming their minds with whole panoplies of sound aphorisms; they must be prompt; they must be crisp; must put some ginger into it; must cut the cackle and come to the horses, the horses being some good, round, eulogistic sentence, readily detachable, for each book's publisher to quote in his advertisements.

It was a bold step. The Education Act was but young. Only a few diners-out had a living hold in those days on the truth that you will talk your best about a book if you know it wholly through the reviews and do not clog your mind or take the sweep and fire out of your conclusions by reading the mere text. But Pinn saw the world steadily and saw it whole. He knew the risk; he knew what ownership of the Stalwart was—a trust for the nation; he knew how wicked, not merely foolish, it would be to stake the solvency of a national institution on the success of an appeal to which the public might, for what he knew, be not yet ripe to answer. Revolving these things, he asked his Muses to send back all books when reviewed, and sold them, the round with the small, at half a crown apiece. Then, fixing the payment for each review at eighteen pence, he felt that the future could be faced.

The bold course proved the wise one. Pinn, kind but firm, schooled his corps of intellectuals till they would fire off considered judgments almost at sight of a binding; none of them but could review a Chinese grammar, the day it came out, and that without giving positive scandal to readers who knew Chinese. The system was thrice blessed. A book was scarcely out before its ravished publisher could cite in his advertisements throughout the island the Stalwart's avowal that once it had taken the volume up it could not lay it down. That did the paper good—trumpeted its name for nothing and broadened its special fame as an organ of culture. Pinn, like a frugal Maecenas, cleared, in some twenty-five years, a couple of thousand pounds by way of the differential shillings alone; and the ladies who sized up all things written must have earned at least enough to find themselves in gas and spectacles. For a thank-offering Pinn spent half of the net gain on a Free Library, set in the heart of a working-class district, a greater boon than he knew to many who, but for it, might have walked far, or waited long, to learn the starting prices.

To this stroke "young George Brumby a youth of fifty summers; the "young" is only to tell Amurath from Amurath—answered with an act of homage to the art of Rembrandt. A Halland architect, John Biggs, had in his wild youth designed the present Warder office, outwardly a scowling pile; within, a powerfully imagined system of draughts and obscurities, as full of cross-lights and tangled glooms as "Hamlet" itself. Its chief glory was the counting-house; no earlier master of Gothic had brought home so well to a body of clerks the savour of life in a well-ventilated mine. In the leisure secured to Bigg by the publicity of this feat—it fronted the Town Hall—the world saw the clerks come blinking out into the sunlight for dinner—he set out, armed solely with the temperament that had undone him in one art, to teach its business to another, though, as one who in stone had created, he scorned to take pay as a critic of other men's un-monumental essays in paint. Until then the Warder had eschewed the valuation of products of art, as a whimsical, womanish job. But the time, Brumby felt, might have come; the man certainly had; and for many years the gifted volunteer made a brilliant figure at the Press Day luncheons where the curators of municipal galleries guide the docile minds of reporters up the crooked paths of critical rightness; this, they will say, was the picture that had to be railed off at the Academy, to keep the crowd away; that was the one the King had seen at Buckingham Palace; that there important canvas was sold already for nine hundred pounds. Biggs, on fire with luncheon and memories of his mighty past, had been known to argue with a curator, and not come off second-best either; awed reporters said so. Even a Biggs can but ripen towards the grave. He grew old; his thoughts took on sombre hues; there always used, he sternly said at one Press view of the Halland Autumn Exhibition, to be a drop of good dry sherry at these times; such decadence in the arts told on him; he fell back, dejected, upon a comparative study of the Wigwam Club's dry sherry and its other vintages; and while Biggs waned, some strange new hand in the Warder waxed, some one who, when he wrote on pictures, had the tone of the true Olympian, the light stoop, the serenity, the air of not being too hard on poor devils drawing on the pavement; no one but Brumby himself, it was thought, could have done it; and then, just as rumour was saying that, it became known that Brumby's own nephew, Dick Sanctuary, heir-presumptive to the paper, had come to join its staff, and had a hobby of this kind of thing. He had, in fact, just over-run Europe, rhapsodizing about pictures, statues, even trinkets, that an English gentleman might, perhaps, have seen with less excitement, his uncle felt; Dick might take no harm, but rather good, by working off this aesthetic craze in the paper before responsibility fell upon him; at bottom the boy was sound; he would come down to earth in good time, and put away childish things.

Childish things, that is, compared with what Brumby, like Pinn, would call "the serious work of the paper," and, again, " the really testing part of journalism"; I mean the fighting down of evil in our public life. Thither, as a Christian publicist, each brought not peace but a sword, or, where a sword would not have been in place, a jet of vitriol, a squirt of weed-killer; for it was careless of me to call them duellists; rather, each was to the other as the snake to the mongoose, or the house rat to the terrier. Not that either mentioned the other. Eatanswill is extinct. Each was true on the whole, to the early British journal's stately faith that none but it was in print, at any rate, anywhere near; nor would either glance, even obliquely, at the other, in the singular number, as "a provincial print"—in less proud cities a paper is felt by an enemy to be a "provincial print" as African is termed by African a "damn black nigger "—much less as "the fish-wrapper," a title, exchanged, as I hear, at need, by two standard-bearers of our culture in the press of the Far East; at most the Stalwart would sniff at some fib set about by "minor organs of the Ministry," or the Warder distinguish from the errors of "Liberals of character" the more starless moral night of " certain Radicals of the baser sort."

Yet, when these salutes were shot, unaddressed, into the ambient ether, Halland knew well enough at whose receivers they were aimed; here was no stage-fight of parties, but a tussle of two strong men; it was Brumby's own thick neck that men saw clothed with thunder in the smashing leaders of the Warder—smashing, but not to Pinn; canst thou make Pinn afraid as a grasshopper? Halland would have known his answering snort among a thousand. When the Stalwart had "seen its dead" and was out to kill in its turn, the glory of its nostrils was terrible to a degree that threw new light on Scripture. Nor was each of them only a party's oriflamme. To the thinker, the man who had heard what a friend had read in a book about Darwin, these sinewy brains, locked in an endless strife, figured the true life of the world, its multitudinous, perfecting quarrels. "I've no politics, bless you," some sportsman would say, "but I like a good old scrap and none of your gloves on," and with lips moving, he would stumble through column-long leaders, chuckling where Brumby got one for his nob, or Bellona's other bridegroom took it on the boko. "I don't say but they're tryers," the very cynic would allow. It was all so English, super-English; only Halland wits—Halland guts, as these plain speakers gleefully said, could have done it. London might melt manhood into courtesies; not these two Halland men. "Dragons of the prime," we felt with awe and pride,

. . . that tore each other in the slime
Were mellow music, matched with them.

CHAPTER II

Blessed influence of one true, loving human soul on another! Not calculable by algebra, not deducible by logic, but mysterious, effectual, mighty.
GEORGE ELIOT

Brumby's editorial room was fit to visit the dreams of a dramatist. Used as a scene, whole ranges of characters could have popped in and out of it all night, and nobody run into anyone else till the good of the play required. For its walls were mainly door; for dooring's sake Wellington, Canning, Dizzy himself (after Millais) were skied; doors to right of him, doors to left of him, at one hand a row of bell-buttons, close as on a page's bosom, at the other a serried squad of mouths of speaking-tubes, Brumby sat like a brain centre in a nervous system—the simile is his; at least, he borrowed it first—feeling at all the threads and living along each fine.

All the evening all the forces of the press, now centripetal and now centrifugal, drew in upon this core to take direction—or were sped outwards from it, aimed and animated. To and from the central, octagonal, sky-lighted room were sucked in or radiated forth, each by his proper door, along the spoke-like corridors, the office messengers with "copy," proofs, letters and telegrams; the foreman, shirt-sleeved, from the composing-room, asking the size of to-morrow's paper; the publisher, not yet perspiring, to know how much per cent. Lord Albry's speech, the thing of tonight, should add on to the parcels for the outer towns; sub-editors doubting how much to make of some not very well-born rumour of a row inside the Cabinet, or if it might be libel, though it were true, to say a borough treasurer had turned invisible since Thursday; the porter from the lift bringing in callers' cards—the Manager, Theatre Royal—would not detain the editor one instant; writer of a letter—turnstiles needed on trams—would the editor see him, simply for five minutes?—reform vital; small deputation from Hospital Friday Committee—had not liked to give him the trouble beforehand to make an appointment; bankrupt of some hours' standing—just two words about to-morrow's report—could nothing be done about the judge's conduct?—method of choosing official receivers, too, thoroughly faulty. Thence would the war correspondent post, at Brumby's bidding, over land and ocean without rest, bent to sweeten the sacred home-life of the Warder's readers with all the heroic pleasures of war, unalloyed by groin wounds or enteric. To this cell, at the heart of the hive, the reporter home from some delicate quest, would come to lay up in the charge of the queen-bee that most perfect-flavoured news which you could never put in the paper.

Now and then you might think the place a ship, and her engines starting; all of it fell a-quivering with a pulse that throbbed up from the embowelled cellarage where, forty feet below the street, the head machineman gave a few trial turns to one of the piled stacks of wheels and cylinders, orchestras of massed inventions, that print and fold, paste and cut, and count out into dozens the best and worst of papers, with an equal hand, like the sun that shines on the just and the unjust. For the moment that sound killed others. It ceased, and then Brumby, as this or that door opened, of all that panelled his room, caught many little busy noises, a whole multitudinous hum, as of June air at noon; the full-volumed whisper from where twelve printers' readers, each in his hutch, read proofs swiftly and low to his mate; the slither of hurrying feet along oil-clothed corridors; near and far off, the click of many typewriters. All the office used type-writers; he wished it; not alone does the master's eye groom the horse; his ear helps.

It helped now. One of the doors—it led to a small room at his back, was half open; through it, as Brumby sat taking his pleasure in that throb and blent hum, the heart's beat, the audible breath, the workaday murmur of life through all the body to which he was brain, there came in the idiom of the speaking typewriter, the cry of a soul in the agonies of literary travail. There would be a sluggish, flagging run of clicks; a pause; a desperate rush at the enemy again, sustained through a brief and feverish fit of clicking; then a stumble, a pause; another fit, shorter; a third, a mere spasm; and then a dying fall, dribbling off into silence that lasted; and then Brumby turned, and eyed with disrelish the nephew in whom the fountains had dried.

Much hung on this Dick. Brumby himself, like Augustus, had been called to empire young. His father, who feared nothing, had started life again, at fifty, as a rural magnate, in a house of icy classic purity, bought at the death—which it hastened—of the great jurist, Lord Dunoustie, long the strength of the

Judicial Committee of the Privy Council, one of the councillors who, the Bible says, "built desolate places for themselves." As Dunoustie was in Fife, it could not be mistaken for the British Museum; that was all you could say for it. For nineteen years the stout old George Brumby bore on fine days the refrigerative sight of its facade, a third of it densely columned portico, impenetrable by light or heat, and on wet days the elegance of a gusty interior where the soul of some raving Edinburgh March seemed to stir in the corpse of a minor Versailles. The mere whistle of domesticated winds was nothing; the genius of Biggs had steeled him for that; it was the lethal chastity of fancy throughout the decoration of this capacious morgue that wore him to a thread before he died.

Others, it may be, but not we
The issue of our toils shall see.

He fell, but the Brumbys were once more "on the land" for which, like good business men on the rise, they had learned the tragic love of Bourbons for lost kingdoms; the county was now all but shooting their grouse; and one neighbour, when nobody Scotch was in hearing, had called old George "Dunoustie," that last happiness; for it he had pitched on Fife and no place in England. To miss such a tide at its flood were to be untrue to oneself as well as to the mighty dead. Dunoustie called to young George. But, first, to find a vicegerent at the Warder, an heir, too, of his state, for none had been born in the very purple. With some tremors he had half fixed on Dick, remembering his own Atlantean toils when at twenty-five he passed from a little racing and some dalliance with the lighter stage, to show the foreman of a great business, which he did not know, the way to go about it. Oh, the run there had been, in bluffing through the first months, on no mean stock of native brass! Could Dick do as much? Was it in him?

You could not say, yet; now a sign told this way, now that. For himself young George had said farewell, a long farewell, to books, in the fifth form at Harrow; of bookishness and the allied taint of uppishness, to which young minds are so exposed at the university, he had a sane dread. Still, Dick did not seem lost. At Oxford, as far as was known, he had diversified a life of rude health with a little reading not conducive to a degree; he rowed in every race he could; at football his brilliance was unquestionable; he had once been all but sent down for helping to burn the Jacobean portion of the Garden Quad, in the gaiety of his youth, on some sufficient occasion. All this counted, and Brumby, who always thought the best of a man till he knew the worst, hoped that at Oxford Dick on the whole had used his time, made good friends, and learnt to carry his wine like a gentleman.

But Dick had fads. One was for a kind of writing; not the right kind; not saying what he had to say and that's an end of it, but a plaguy, itchy fussing over some phrase, planing it down or bevelling it off, inlaying it with picked words of a queer far-fetched aptness, making it clang with whole pomps of proper names, that boomed into their places, like drums and cymbals in symphonies, or twinkle and tingle, shot with ironies, or rise and fall like a voice that means more by the tune than the words; apish tricks, held in distaste by his uncle, in whom good sense and right feeling burned with a flame too eager and quick to let him dally with forms. There was Dick, at this moment, grunting and sweating and sticking fast a dozen times; all this in a little picture-notice that a journalist who knew his work would turn off in ten minutes. Why, if it came to that, was he doing such things at all? Brumby was no Philistine, he had the best wall of Turners in Halland. But he knew work from play. "We must bring him on," he felt; Dick must be weaned from these finicking aesthetics. With Brumby, to will an end was to pounce, next thing, on some means to it. Office messengers came in and went out, almost ceaselessly, on silent soles. The next to come brought a low pile of crinkling sheets of tissue paper pinned together.
"Lord Albry's speech, sir," the boy said, handing it.

"Ah," said Brumby, with such gusto as decency allowed before the menial. Lord Albry was rhetorician-in-chief to the party. And then Brumby had an idea.

"Last slips?" he asked.

"Yes, sir. Connelusion, sir."

Released with a nod, the boy left the presence.
With the "flimsy" unread in his hand, Brumby turned to where Dick was tilting his chair on its hind legs and malevolently eyeing, from the distance thus attained, the abortive heir of his invention.

"Dick," Brumby called, in the tone of the senior at ease in his beneficence.

"Uncle?" Dick's eyes looked up, not his care-eaten mind.

Brumby beckoned Dick to a chair near his and passed him the sheaf of rustling leaves. It was inordinate promotion. Dick, though of the blood, was the rawest acolyte; what other high priest would have had him on a night like this, into the Holy of Holies? But Brumby always had said that what others might think quixotic he found, as often as not, to be the true prudence.

"Read it out, will you?" he said to Dick.

Dick's eyes groped vacantly over the pencilled film.

"Warder, Halland," he began, without life, at the first words he found written.

"Yes, yes." Brumby tapped the edge of his desk, conductor-fashion, with his hexagonal blue pencil. "It's addressed to us of course. But the speech, man, the speech." He spoke with a judge's contained and purposeful impatience. Really the boy should have learnt by now to give his mind to what he was at. Dick's mild and magnificent eye travelled slowly to the point where the pencil hit the desk. If you tried to bustle Dick at his work, he just laid down the work and, unhasting, unresting, took in the idea of bustle. It was quite respectful; it might be reverent; but it made you a conscious phenomenon. So a twinge of discomfort traversed the uncle. Take a man as you find him though; that was one of his rules. "All right, my boy," he said with re-fixed good humour, "you'll soon learn."

For a moment more the pensive lustre of Dick's gaze rested on the point of contact of the two woods. Some lights are turned on sooner than off. Then it withdrew, unhurried, to the flimsy and made casts over its surface. "Ah, this will be it," he said at last, glad to do what was wished.

Brumby's feet were only just kept from drumming a peremptory tune by his certainty that, if they did so, two large pools of luminous darkness would, after a short period of adjustment, be reposing on them, framing a conception of them. So he merely said, "Well?" and then Dick read aloud, without dramatic intention or fire; indeed he made all run into one—the current voice of the great man and the interjections wrung from the bosoms of his audience; the tone was the same; only a slight jolt announced Dick's discomfort when the thread broke at either end of these improvisations.

"'And now,'" he read out, "'I have done—(cries of "No, no," and "Go on")—all but this last word; be one people (Cheers); have no parties.'"

"Eh? Eh?" queried Brumby, uneasy. No nonsense, he hoped, from Albry, of all men.

"'Root up the weeds of faction—yes—(Cheers).'"

"Ah!" Brumby breathed. This looked more like.

"'Purge the dross, the unpatriotic, undutiful dross, out of Parliament—yes—(Cheers).'"

"Good!" Brumby rose, quite relieved; he must stand with his back to the fire. The first nip of verbal strong waters worked in him visibly; as Dick read, his uncle's face, his body, his clothes became charged with expression; firmly and ever more firmly he planted himself on the rug; swiftly, as ideas opened out, he undid all the buttons of his frock-coat; relentlessly, as the relentless logic closed in, nail by nail, he did them up; as the peroration burst into view he threw an ascending series of chests and glared terribly at the umbrella-rack, coal-box and other points where holders of dissimilar views might be conceived as attempting a last stand.

"'Keep down,'" Dick's voice trailed on, unstirred, "'the vermin of politics—yes—(Renewed cheers).'"

"Strong, that!" said Brumby with a gusto the least bit dubious; he was great on the decencies of public life. "Still"—there was a moment's struggle; then he relinquished the attempt to carry charity to lengths vetoed by reason—"they are vermin, most of these latter-day Radicals, literally."

"Literally?" Dick's eyes swung round on their axis; there was speculation in them now; the 'prentice wordsman, intent as a child on the mystery, questioned the face of his elder in the craft; not demurring; simply wanting to know. "Literally?"

To Brumby, now soaring in bluest vaults of generous passion, technique was as clay. Base was the slave who parsed; no man, but a worm, he who defined his terms. But it was, to be fair to him, not in his mind to impute to his own flesh and blood so grovelling an interest. The lad, he felt, was just wondering, could the world be so bad?

"My boy," Brumby began with gentle firmness; he would hold Dick's arm while he showed him the pit. Then he checked. No; better spare the boy while he could. "Well, well, you'll know soon enough. Yes?" Dick was to read on. His eyes, with the wonder still in them, revolved back to the telegram. "'And thus, and thus only, be one people (Loud cheers). I fear this is no popular doctrine I give you. Well, I give it (Renewed cheers). And now do as you will. Punish me; drive me, if you wish, from public life. I can bear it. I can, I trust, bear anything but the thought that I had kept from you, at this hour of all hours in our nation's life, one jot of such truth as may be in me (Tremendous cheering, during which Lord Albry resumed his seat, having spoken for an hour and ten minutes).'"

"Now, there's a man," said Brumby, when he could trust his voice.

At the words a new wonder shone out of Dick—not dissent; only a wish to be taught. "To—to stand that rot—cheering and all that?"

"Rot!" Brumby stared. What morbid freak was it now?

"I mean—well, of course anyone would feel a fool, being buttered up, that way. You mean, he didn't shirk it?"

Talk like this made Brumby feel as if fissures, going down to the waters under the earth, were opening between his feet. "Think, think," he said sharply, "think what the man has at stake." "Oh!" said Dick, almost hurriedly—friendly soul, he hated to vex people; when he lost touch he would make rushes this way and that, if perchance he might meet them half-way. "You mean there's the risk of—of what might be thought of him—giving that mob what it liked, that way?"

Brumby's voice grew austere, almost pinched, a strange thing for it. "Is it really possible," he asked, "that you did not grasp what Lord Albry said of being driven from public life?"

"Was it," said Dick, only wanting to concur, if he could see with what—and you know, he had not quite given his mind to what he read—"was it—he felt he couldn't go on for ever at this sort of thing—of course he'd hate it, anyone would—getting up that way and telling a crowd, to its face, that it's right?" It was clearly a case for a talking-to. Yet Brumby was not glad, wholly. Nothing was more to his mind as a rule, than public speaking, in private; that was the true nectar, with no fly in it; the real thing, real in the bald and rigid sense, was like the Greek triremes of war to which, we are told, many fortunate flukes had to happen before they would act; he must have had wine enough, but only enough; all must go well with the early joke, broad, genial, and humane, at which the audience should warm with a sense that he too, high as he stood, was a man and a brother; till, at least, he had played himself in, the cheers must come all right at each appointed place, the purple patch at the close of each clause, freely enough to let him run over, without looking stuck, the heads of the next on a card in the palm of his hand; but based on a hearthrug, man could dominate his world; with the cashier, or a young reporter, or even with as close approximations to a hero's valets as his wife and daughter, hanging on his lips, Brumby felt he could make them hang, and he liked it.

But Dick was a disconcerting lump to address; not lumpish, strictly; a graceful mass, a great stalking athlete from a Greek frieze; you might feel him crazy, but not null; docile too, in a way; as often as Brumby came out with some crystal of practical wisdom, the slowly formed gains of a lifetime, or handed to Dick some holograph chart, his own work, of the shoaly seas of thought upon life and conduct, upon business, manners and the arts, Dick would listen with rounding eyes, silent or only putting in, here and there, a question that opened up new reaches to be buoyed out by the pilot mind; and yet—well, to change the figure, it seemed as if some fine pile of rock had asked nothing better of Moses than just to be smitten and have its miraculous waters drawn from it, and Moses had smitten, and then found the rod would not bite on that special formation of rock; there are feathers, again, that a pellet will glance off; in Dick's willingness to learn, the most unerring shafts of the elder's sagacity buried themselves and were lost, like bullets fired into penetrable-looking sand. Still, a man must try; it was only fair to the boy, and to the paper.

"My dear boy," Brumby began, with only the faintest presentient note of deflation in the full tone, "to be warned, once for all, against morbid refining on what are, I assure you, the clearest things in the world—the dictates of right feeling, and common sense. Dick, now that your manhood has come, I do beseech you, pull yourself together; keep a fast hold on the things that do matter in life—the great sanities, the great simplicities of life. All honour, I say"—and now the voice, heartened by his ear, rang out nobly—"to Lord Albry that he keeps in touch with all that is best in our people. All honour, I say again, to our people's hearts if they know, and show that they know, a man when they see him."

Brumby's chest, always good, was superbly convex as he finished this exordium, with his coat entirely buttoned up, and severely tried at the buttons, and his planted legs almost columnar in aspect with the grandeur of his spirit. Ah, had Dick been a full drill-hall, clapping! But there he sat, a statue, heroic size, of balked desire to be thrilled, sure that it must be something real that one who knew so much better had got hold of; but, beyond that, immersed in perplexity. While the orator contended with a shiver, there came a diffident tap at a door. "Confound!" said the orator's voice, but his heart said: "Thank God!" "Come in," he shouted, and then, as the opening door was peered round by a diffident face, "Oh! You, Fay? Come in, my dear fellow."

CHAPTER III

And whereso'er such lord is found, such client still will be.
MACAULAY

Fay looked, say, thirty-three; he had eyes like a nice beast's, shy but not savage, a mouth all a twitch with responsiveness to anyone's mood; mobile colour; and, just where in English faces the firmly blank chins are, a waiting alphabet of meaning dimples, to be marshalled by each moment's emotion into copious scriptures of expression. He walked as on sufferance, offering the ground, with manifest misgivings, the refusal of himself; the foot, as he entered now, did not take the floor plump, like a free man's; it hung, it fumbled at the oilcloth, every touch a "Beg your pardon," or "Am I a nuisance?" said in the idiom of gait.

You might, off-hand, have said, either "Sheepish lout!" or "Parasitic fraud!" and been wrong in either. Working bps, fidgety eyes, all the quick, weak, clever sensibility that flickered about the face and braced and slackened off the limbs as the eyes took light or caught a chill from somebody else's look of spirit or shiver of misgiving—these were enigmatic till you guessed that they came of two things, distinguishable, a gift and a knack of using it. First there was, playing its authentic melodies of self-expression on the eyes and mouth and the tunable blood in the cheeks, the Celt's—one breed of Celt's—shy ardour of longing to understand you, please you, concur with you. Then, over those kind fires, there watched, furtive, alert, defensive, a sense of their use for ends not themselves. Sympathy was a passion; yet, in the thick of its tumults, a wariness had found means to live; you espied it, at moments, through the whirl, sitting contained, secure, conceivably gleeful.

"Come in, Fay," Brumby iterated, "come in."

To a burly British heartiness a touch of almost anxious cordiality was added as he greeted this exotic. Dick found he was thinking—" Strange! What good can he be to my uncle?" The critic in Dick had begun.

"Why, I don't believe," the genial voice was rolling on, "you and my nephew Dick have met."

The younger men bowed; the Irishman awed, as his way was, by any complete stranger's force of mind and beauty of soul. Dick marvelled more calmly; in these days, like the Jews in the Bible, he often marvelled greatly; yet he had on a rind, still, of the fuss-shunning public school-boy; it made him, outside, seem blent of the lofty soul in Aristotle's ethics, to whom "nothing was so very great," and the first man, on the first clear night, with the moon and stars about him.

"Mr. Fay, as you know—" Brumby's voice again; for a second the others had met in a quiet of their own; now a settled blue-bottle seemed to take wing; it broke into the tete-a-tete. "Mr. Fay, as you know, is my confidential secretary, and, if he will bear my saying so"—he put a fatherly hand on the shoulder of each—"as fine a model for a young English journalist as any you'll find in the Press."

"Please, please!" Fay spluttered, and then his eyes, in trying to wriggle out of their sockets with confusion, hit again upon Dick's, and abode there, moored to he could not tell what. While Brumby buzzed on, almost defiant in his stress on his own zeal to praise where praise was due, each looked past or through him and some way into the other, and distantly signalled a wish to look further.

"I say," Brumby rounded to a close, "as any in the British Press. And now," he broke off, "for shop."

Dick took it that he was done with; his parturient genius, he supposed, might now return to the privacy from which it had been summoned. No such thing. "Rest a while, Dick," came his uncle's voice like a clap on the shoulder; "stay here a bit, my boy; high time we let you into 'the secrets of the prison-house!'"

In Brumby's elocution any quotations he made were fenced round with audible inverted commas and closed with a note of exclamation gigantic beyond the power of print to express. This served three good ends; it drew your mind to his command of literature; it reassured you—told you that, with him, lapses from the virile, literal use of words were not the rule; and it warned you fairly that the matter quoted must be taken as it stood, with all its faults, the vendor not being the maker. At this voluminous note on the poor old tag, Dick's eyes again, by some chance, ran up against Fay's; not a wince of disloyalty was there either in the nephew's or the right-hand man's; both looks were virginally blank; still, they met. Dick sat back in a chair, at the receipt of ideas; Brumby, from his state on the hearthrug, turned, every inch the able editor, to Fay; Fay under the Jovian eye, shuffled on the oilcloth, leant, for countenance, on the edge of the table, and crumpled or wrung out visionary caps between his fingers. All looked excellent in their parts.

"The leader to-night, of course—" Brumby began.

"Only one subject possible—seems to me," Fay abruptly cut in. At the other's "Of course," he went off like a gun; from that instant you saw—Brumby saw—that Fay had come charged with explosive personal conviction on the point, so that even at his liege lord he must let fly, if opposed, and spare not. You may stroke pretty hard, if you stroke the right way.

"As you say," purred Brumby, "Lord Albry's speech. You've read the report?"

"Not to the very end," said Fay. He had not, in fact, read a word; had not known, till now, that Lord Albry was speaking. But he made it his care to let cats out of bags, and genies from their leaden pots, by very minute instalments; a fingernail, or the tip of an ear, enough to begin with; freedom, time to look round, to draw back, these he must have. "Cut losses and let profits run"; the children of this world, investing in that which is dross, make a practice of that; how much more needful the liberty to do so when the venture is in stuff precious and perilous, like candour.

Brumby handed the flimsy. "There you are!" he said. Fay dropped an eye from the head to the foot of each page. Then he looked up. "Well?" Brumby asked.

"Well, for my own part" Fay said and paused. What need, his face said, of words? Pursed lips, raised brows, a speaking shrug—the plastic clay had set; it offered an image symbolic of strength of opinion. Brumby purred again. "I thought you'd be struck. What's this though? Oh, another slip; it's the last; I mislaid it." Fay's eye swiftly descended it, too.

"Eh?" Brumby asked.

"Well, personally I—" But no. Of what use to speak? Strong men are still men; words fall so far short of their rugged individual sense of the impossibility of any view but the one. Fay, as he stopped, opened both palms, almost Gallically, with a little laugh. "I must really give you up," it seemed to say, "if you're not sound on this."

So Brumby took it. "I knew you'd feel that," he said; and again, with an inculcative glance at Dick, "knew it." Ah, had Dick such conviction!

"Something like, eh?" he went on to Fay, with a nod towards the speech.

Fay had read scarcely a word; he had not had time; who can read and fence too, in a moment? Better to pick out of Brumby both what was said in the speech and what must be written about it. All Fay did was to take up the key-note of gusto. "Hits pretty hard," he said, with enjoyment, " does Albry. Still—" Again he pulled up; enough if he turned the leaf; not for him to fill the new page; he handed Brumby the pencil.

Brumby took it. "Still, as you say, not too hard. Well, now it's our turn. Frankly, now, what shall we say in the leader?"

Fay, like other tall spirits, was most himself when most pressed. Any of your common fungoid growths on greatness would have halted, stammered, vowed it was not for him to say. The stumping question was always the one that Fay dealt with most patly. "Why," he said promptly, "if you should leave it to me," and again no words were sweeping enough; again a gleaming blank page was held out to the itching pencil.

"I confess," said Brumby gravely, "I entirely agree."

Fay fished away tranquilly. "Of course, if Albry hits out, we—"

The fish did its duty. "Precisely," said Brumby. "We must hit too, and hard. Whatever it cost, that brave man must not stand alone."

That was clear, then; Albry was still to be backed; lately his vogue had not been quite what it was; and Brumby was no sentimentalist; no one less likely than he to go about bowing to suns that were unmistakably setting; Albry's, it seemed, was still high enough in the sky; he was the man, and wisdom would die with him. Turns for the better in many crises like this had disciplined Fay's jaws and gullet; he could swallow a sigh of relief as clean as the well-bred will eat up a hiccough. One was being thus privily consumed when, from the ignored, forgotten Dick, came the one word, round and full as an astonished eye—"Alone!"

Little as Fay had looked at Lord Albry's speech, still he had just caught a glimpse of that nobleman martyred with volleys of roses, and holding out faithfully unto that end. He liked such spectacles. So his eyes and Dick's met again, and each understood; there was reticence still, but a reticence, now, that stated the theme of its silence; and then they heard, like a noise in the street when you talk indoors, Brumby's voice, now cross, breaking in on that tacit exchange of perceptions, and measuring too how far he was barred out from having a part in it. "Dick, I understood you were to write a notice of the Mountain Painters' Exhibition."

How beastly percipient, Dick felt, the beggar's face was; nothing, indeed, distinct enough to resent in the sense that there was in Fay's eyes of the meanness of hinting that Dick was neglecting the work from which the hinter had kept him; not a twinkle, not a long look, even; and, yet, instant, complete comprehension. Among these three—between, also, any two of them—there were exclusions, concessions, sufferances, ironies, not understood altogether by Dick, not understood at all, he was coming to think, by his uncle. This Fay understood all; see him now, where he stood shuffling, colouring, hanging out every signal of sheepish discomfort and no empty signals either; discomfort was there; and yet, with it, a wit that played at its ease, stripped them naked, and took in the turns of their minds like so many diaphanous ruses of children. However, Dick was back in his room, to meditate the thankless muse.

"Sorry to put it on to you," said Brumby to Fay, "but do you think you could write on Albry to-night?"

"I'll try, if you wish it."

"The truth is I have a rather big Church Schools Protection Committee to-night"—he looked at his watch—"by Jove, I must bolt to it."

This, or some allied truth, was a homage that Brumby would commonly pay, of a night, to self-love. To be easy, he had to be sure it was something quite out of the way if he hurled any lightning not quite his own make. The time Fay had been forging him bolts now ran into years, but the freshness of Brumby's first sense of only just leaving his post for a moment or so was still unabated; each night there would fall, to his unhidden disappointment, some chance that took the pen from his hand; each night, as he asked Fay to write in his stead, there thrilled in his voice the fears of a Napoleon, forced at a critical hour to turn over everything to a lieutenant, one who is capable, who will do his best, but is not Napoleon. At the committees too—and they multiplied, for the bossing of good works is like dram-drinking—chances of much the same kind had a way of befalling. When the talking gave out, and work was at hand, Brumby used to be torn from the board by the outcries of his duty to the Warder. As this, in a man of his mettle, proved his toils for the paper more exacting than the most exacting tasks of the body he relinquished, all its members felt what a terrible life an editor's was. As he left the Warder too, when its need was the sorest, its staff were touched by the measure this gave of the appalling severity of calls which outweighed a confessed preference for the more to the less trying parts of journalism. So his fame grew at both ends; having several working-places to leave when anything had to be done with a will in any of them, he gained the name of a man who did with all his might whatsoever his hand found to do. And that reputation was sacred in his sight; it never lacked, at the right time, like this, the offering of a few properly chosen words.

No acolyte could like, better than Fay did, the fun of swinging the censer and watching the celebrant priest as he made the oblation. When Fay gave his response, his "I'll try, if you wish it," the tone was one that the celebrant Brumby would snuff up like myrrh. It conveyed all the essential truth of the matter; that Fay's lips would be put to the mouthpiece of the megaphone just for this once, by way of experiment, probably unsuccessful, but less so than if he had not Brumby's example, Brumby's spirit, to animate him so strongly that, indeed, in no profound or philosophical sense could Fay, or anything but Brumby, be said to be there at all.

"Could you write here to-night?" Brumby asked.

"In your room?" Fay stressed the "your" delicately. "I, a writer, mind camping on Helicon?" the stress said, without being fulsome.

Brumby designated his own chair. "It won't put you off?" he asked with complacent humility.

"Not it!" Fay laughed lucidly. Apollo's own seat put him off! He would fetch his typing machine in a moment.

Would he mind too, asked Brumby, glancing through Dick's notice, when done, and sending it up to be set; he, Brumby, would see it in proof—would be back by midnight, he hoped, bat might be kept later. Dick, he ought to explain, after a week of trial in harness, was leaving that night by the midnight train for a fortnight in the Lakes.

"And I want you to tell me frankly, just what you think of the boy's work before he is finally put on the staff." In just such a whisper might Haroun al-Raschid have bidden the trusty, the lowly Mesrour take a look at the latest thing in the way of a likely heir to the Caliphate.

Yes, Mesrour would try. He went out to fetch his plant. And then, through the other open door, Brumby eyed the labouring Dick, with a look compounded of many ingredients—distaste for the crank, the freak, the inopportunist, frozen when it was time to flow, fluent in unprofitable interjections when it was time to refrain from flowing; and dynastic instinct and hope; and affection for his sister's son; and then, again, jealousy for his own son, who had not been born. "Dick," he called pretty genially, going to him.

"Uncle?" The answer came out of cavernous depths of absorption. Dick had again got far from the Brumbys and Fays of this world; he bore, in a dark of his own, the dear agonies of artists who have not a method, and want one—saw, with sweats and aches of desire, the vanes on spires he could envisage, but not build—only fumble about the formless bases of thoughts that, could they be given their rights, would spring clean up at the sky, all the world's grace in one jet, lifted on all the world's strength.

"Good-bye, Dick. May not see you again—that's if you're done early, as I hope." His eye upbraided the mean issue of Dick's travail. "Ah, you should just see Fay put a job through when he's driven." A valedictory hand enjoined Dick's shoulder; " Model yourself on him, my boy. Not on me. On him!"

CHAPTER IV

Your young men shall see visions.

In the creative mind, as well as in other places, the wind bloweth where it listeth. In Dick's it was now to blow great guns, but not ones that held. Heady gusts of clicking would drop down into lulls of some length, painfully traversed by straggling single files of ticks; and these light airs would die right away to dead calms, or again be whipped up into fresh squalls that had a keep-it-up-or-else-we're-done-for clatter about them, as if a horse were trying to rush a hill too steep for the weight in the cart. The spirit bloweth and is still.

Where Fay sat there was continuous peace; not one click was his typewriter asked for. Brumby gone, he had sent for the whole report of Lord Albry's speech; but not to read through; he glanced at two or three pages picked at random; then, as if these samples had merely confirmed some previous estimate of the value of rhetoric in bulk, he plumped down on the whole pile of volatile tissue a monumental paper-weight, round the outer edge of which it rose mantling and reaming like some fluffy ghost fighting the stake run through its vitals to lay it, while Fay took from a pocket several small bundles of typewritten papers, chose one maturely, and putting back the rest, looked critically through it, taking his ease in his chair and laying down page after page on the table, when read.

Once or twice, when Dick's pangs were more poignantly articulate than usual, Fay looked through the door, and moved uneasily, as you will see a cat, when a baby cries, uncurl from her sleep at the fire, fidget, and gurgle, compelled by her matronly bowels of compassion. Nothing but this had yet marred the Sabbatical calm in the editor's room, or interrupted the tempest in Dick's, when, twenty minutes after Brumby had left, there fell on Fay's ears, resonant and abrupt, like some surprise visit from conscience, the question:

"How the deuce d'you come to do it?"

Dick was throwing one of his bombs again. And how could you know it was harmless? So Fay, who was not a soldier of fortune for nothing, rushed in to pick up the bomb and throw it away; at the first word his hand had gone with a jump to his typewriter's keyboard; by the time that Dick's last word was out, the machine was well in its stride. "Pardon, one moment," he said, not thinking what he said; just the instinctive first pass of a fencer set upon in the dark and striking out anyhow till he find his guard. Or, say, he typed as if every word typed were a spadeful of earth and he had to throw up an earthwork breast high or be taken. "You said?" he asked, when first he could rest on his spade.

"What beats me's how you ever learnt this sort of trick?"

"Trick?" But, in Fay, histrionic resentment was never first-rate. Some imp in him, some traitor inside the walls, would run a pin into a gasbag of his own inflating, in his hour of need, as soon as if it were somebody else's.

"Trick? Knack then. D'you want it called accomplishment?" Dick grimaced, and again their minds met in a wince at the impossible word. "I mean how on earth do you turn to and write straight on, when you have to?"

Was that all? Relief had again to consume its own smoke. "Oh, you leave off your damnable faces and begin," Fay said inspiritingly.

"But—when you care?" said Dick. "When the thing, that you're writing on, matters?"

"Ah?" said Fay, piqued by the change of topic. He sat back, his face all kind eyes and pricked ears. Dick had come near; he sat on a corner of the table, his big thighs flattened out to gigantic widths; Fay admired them.

" It's like this—" Dick began, and then panic seized the thought that had seemed to have so much in it till the time came to leave the warm, dark place of its birth in the mind. It held back in fright, lest it be like one's wit, that so flashed and rang in a dream, till you awoke and, lo, it was gibberish. Fay lit a pipe. Lucina's self can do no more, on these occasions.

Dick plunged. "I saw the earth made, this July." Fay nodded, the understanding not of wise child to wise child. Dick was helped. "It was in the Valais; we were climbing. You know the sort of thing?"

" No." The tone said "Tell me."

"You pig half the night in a hut, some way up, at the edge of the snow. At, say, two, you get up and go on. By Jove, it's still. You can hear every little whispering whistle of a wind that can't stir a thing, it's so small—only go leaping about in the dark, doing nothing. There's always a torrent a mile off in the valley; you go up and up and the noise of it thins away to a sort of hum of thought about some noise there used to be—you know the way, when you're going asleep, the thud in the street drones off into a dream about it. Next thing you look up with a start; the front man has stopped to put out the lantern, but ever so far off, over the Rhone, there's a grave, russet light being held to the face of sleeping provinces."
"'Held to the face of sleeping provinces.' H'm," said Fay, "it scans. All right otherwise. I say, though, provinces? What about cantons?"

"Cantons? Hang it, no. That murders it. Provinces." It was the first time that Dick had ever stood up for a wording of his own, not to say one he did not know the case for. To his amazement, Fay saw—in fact, had only feared lest Dick had preferred the good tune to the bad by an accident.

"Of course it's 'provinces,'" said Fay, delighted. "Go it."

Dick did. "Next all that side of the earth lets down with a dip, and the sun sets off, right up the sky. He has spiky rays sticking out all round. The whole thing looks naked and sore at first—eye with no eyelids —that sort of feel. Then our mountain fired his morning gun—first fall of rock, you know, for the day— crash into that staring, straining silence, like a stone gone bang into a window. That did it for me; something gave; it got out of the way; just for a second I fit on God, or whoever it is, going on with the earth. He'd the frost in one hand and that flame in the other; had been ramming in wedges of ice all night, to split up the stone, and was going round now and picking 'em out with the sun and tilting the night's take of scree down into the valley to add to the made earth He has there. There I was, right in the forge; my own body shook, where I stood, with the fall of the hammer that beats out the world."

Dick's eye, rolling either from heaven to earth, or else back again, caught Fay's midway. Fay's was as gravely and simply intent as could be asked by one in whom there was thawing at last the long frost in which we bind, with so much care, the wits of the picked youth of Britain. It is a shy business, however, this first wild attempt to be human, for one duly schooled in the ethics of petrifaction. They ought to have been in the dark. Dick checked; the puissant thigh, pressed on the table edge, ceased by turns to flatten out and swell up curvilineally, rhythmically, to the swing of the leg below. Obstipuit retroque pedem cum voce repressit. "I can't think," Dick said, rather grim, "why I'm telling you all this."

"I can't think," Fay responded, "why I knew you'd say it when you started."

Both, again, had the looks of friends that grope, with a faith in something to find.

"Perhaps," said Dick, disarming, "that's why I'm telling you."

"Well?" Fay puffed Lucina's pipe.

"Well," resumed Dick; but it took some more words of his own to bring back the right heat; "that one second I had my hand on the thing; only, I couldn't hold it; it just came slipping across some line, the way stars twinkle into sight and out again, and then it was gone, and the way the earth is made, and moved, and all, were no better than ever—just the old, dead, rotten truths in books. But d'you know, I fancy these beggars who paint—the best of 'em—just stick like that; I believe they're not kept out of the big finds at all; they can go on all day coming on the fact that snow's white, and sky blue, and that mothers like their babies, and so on, and yelling ' Bags I! ' at each thing they spot, as if they'd never been set upon at school and shown it was too much of a truism to have the shiny loveliness of being true. They can put us others up to it too. Do you know the best feel in the world? Oh, no, you said you didn't. Well, it's one special sting on your cheek, the sting of blown granules of ice on a high pass at dawn. I only found that out to-day. More of me felt it, at one of these pictures, than ever got near it all over the Alps."

He took breath. He had to. Fay, to leave no stillness for ice to re-form in, murmured the worn lines from Browning:

"For, don't you mark? we're made so that we love
First, when we see them painted, things we have passed
Perhaps a hundred times, nor cared to see;
And so they are better, painted—better to us,
Which is the same thing. Art was given for that."

"That's it," said Dick, a little surprised, as you are at that age, to find that anyone else had felt what you feel, and not pulled the whole place down to show it. "That beggar knew, who wrote that. I put in four hours raising my eyes from the dead to-day, at that show. Whole minutes I wasn't blind at all, and, the times I saw, I saw myself seeing; part of me sat and watched the millions of tiny waves—you know the notion—come in and break on shores in my eyes, and bring me my own, home. But—what to write!" He was fluent now, even in gesture; floods follow frost in these waters, as in others. "What to write!" he repeated, unparalyzed by the sound of an interjection, a three-word interjection, from his own lips; and his whole body, once a public school boy's, signalled despair.

"Why not just that?"

" That rant about myself?" One note of interrogation superimposed on two of exclamation, might give a rough quantitative analysis of Dick's tone into its ingredients of inquiry and horror.

"Art is about oneself," said Fay. "Still—"

Fay's voice hung for a moment.

Dick could not wait. "Still? Yes?"

"If you prefer the alternative—" and Fay raised the voice of some cheerless wader in ponds of dull print, and recited with dragging lifelessness—"'The thirteenth'—give me the catalogue." Dick handed over an exhibition catalogue in slip proof, a cascade of wriggling coils of paper. Fay looked, and went on. "No; 'The Fifteenth Annual Exhibition of Mountain Paintings by British Artists at the City Art Gallery may fairly be said to be marked, on the whole, by a higher level of achievement than—'" He looked a query at Dick.

"Oh, august muck like that?" said Dick, with some curiosity. He had seen magisterial trash of the sort, but not in the making. Still, his valuation of the product was quite decipherable.

"Rant away, then," said Fay benignly. "Or," he went on, "would this do? The scholarly line, sir, the scholarly. 'Sir Joshua's precept that Art must "see large" has clearly—'"

"You've seen the show, then?" Dick interrupted.

"Ex-officio. I'm a journalist, and ex-offiicio I've seen everything."

"You've not seen it?"

Fay pursued, with untwinkling eyes: "'—has clearly been taken to heart by the best of our younger men.'" He looked across. Did Dick want any more?

"Well, you can forge!" Dick marvelled.

"You can't," Fay retorted, "so rant, like an honest boy. There!"

He threw Dick the bunch of twirling tails. Fay, towards the end, had talked at his ease; sheepishness had left him. The bravest man, in the most respectable way, may not be his full self while he is safe; it takes a good big risk, with some of these Bayards, to kill off the minor terrors that bully their souls; you cannot feel shy while the house is on fire, nor be quelled, as you were, by a wart on the nose, with the ship going down. You come up to speak to some danger and find what it means to be let off your everyday fears of speaking with friends. Fay's look and voice, while he toyed with possibilities of roguish daring, had the calm of the braced hero's. And yet he was weak; as Dick went back to his toils with a dismissive "Thank you" for what Fay had offered, in the sure hope of its rejection, Fay's assured ease died out of his face, to have its place soon taken by womanish ruth at the look of Dick's bent head, which was nice, brown, curly, and troubled. For a minute the dykes held; then a new unreserve, new in kind, broke through with a rush:

"Ah, then, spill it out any way, just as it comes; why not, and you after seeing just what they're about, there, in spite of the paint? Anny way that it comes. No one'll think that it's good, in this place, but you'll still have the soul in you left, and the sight of an eye in your head, and that's something."

The trail and swing of the rhythms of Irish speech, now let go by Fay for the first time, were what took Dick most. But the glance at "this place" could still stiffen the nephew in him. So "Thank you" was all he said, again, though not quite as before; and again he fell to work, trying to rush the glass hill. Each time that he charged a few feet up it, each time that he slithered back with a run, each time he rested to rub his bruises, the typewriter issued its bulletin, audible or silent.

Fay, too, bent himself up to his task. He looked through a few more typed pages, wrote in a word or two, and then rang. "That's the whole of the leader," he said, giving the bundle to the messenger who came in answer. "This can go, too." He pointed to the weighted pile of tissue paper, the great man's speech; and the messenger hurried away with the double haul of forage for the linotype machines ravening in the attic. Out of the same teeming pocket as before, Fay selected a second small bundle of typed sheets, and began to go through it like the other, but very warily, somewhat as sparrows feed under windows.

Half an hour went; in the streets the spaces of silence lengthened and the few sounds left rose into high and higher relief on their background of stillness; a four-wheeler's iron tyres brutally scrunched on the setts; nails in the boots of a solitary passer rang on the flags; over the way a tavern closed its back door; the last Bacchanal to issue, propelled by some hand, could be heard in the windless night asserting the dignity of years—"Lemme alone. I'm an old man. Gimme a drink. Lemme alone"; then quiet, once ripped right into, far off, by some street-girl's mirthless squeal of laughter; dotted, too, for a while, with a light periodic spatter on stone, from where a tuberculous subject stood on the kerb, expectorating, till he shuffled off, holding his shoes on by continuous contact with the pavement, to find a dry arch for the night. Then full, circling silence that seemed almost ancient when across its outer rim there thrilled into hearing the one high note of heroic romance in sleeping cities, the first smash of the gong of a horsed fire-escape; twenty seconds more and it had rushed crashing up the scale of clearness to an instant glory of torch-light and galloping hoofs in the street below, and then down the other side and out over the edge of the crossed orb of stillness.

Fay sucked in the divine sound. A big fire, perhaps; the roof gone; inside the four black walls a homogeneous hell, a cubical crater tossing up burning logs like so many sparks, or reaching across streets with sixty-foot tongues of flame, their tips uncurling as they went, like tape from a fallen reel, to lick off the paint on the woodwork of opposite windows. Circumstantial imagination was rapture; but agony, not to be there. Fay had the appetites of youth. What a corpse or an ambulance is to a healthy child, even that was a house on fire to him—its sight an ultimate good, to be sought and feasted upon with as single a fervour, recalled with as wholly thankful a heart for its coming his way, and all without any failure of compassion for the house-holder or the deceased.

Dick, like that other boy whom the transit of Venus could not interest, had not so much as looked up while this meteoric clatter traversed the night's firmament of quiet. Fay, confronted with this instance of distraction from the sane quest of a practicable happiness, was just thinking, like Burke, what shadows we are and what shadows we pursue, when Dick abruptly illustrated the reflection by rising with a face sombred with youth's most adequate sense of the length, breadth and depth of its own tragedy.

"So?" said Fay to himself, understanding. "Ter frustra, comprensa," he quoted aloud, in a cheerful interrogative, "mantis effugit imago? Eh?"

Dick was past capping quotations. "I'm done," he said, making for his hat-peg darkly.

"Stick it again a bit, eh?" Fay asked. A nice fix, this, for him that had never felt senior to anyone living. It looked, for all the world, like a case for coming the elder brother.

Dick was squashing the birth-strangled babe in one hand. "Stick? It won't. It just slops out of me—mushy, washy, gush—here and there a word means"—for a second the crumpling was stayed—"but the rest—ugh!" And Dick crushed the object of scorn into a harder ball.

"Young 'un"—Fay began, with difficulty. How, he tried to recall, did the volunteer elder brothers do it, in English literature? Come to think of it, what was Pendennis' stoop like, with Clive? How did Warrington warm to his lengthened, sage advices? For one thing, the younger brothers stood still to be stooped to. Dick didn't. He put on his hat.

"Will you tell my uncle," he said, " I've failed again?"

"Again?"

"You don't know? Of course not. Same thing the first try I had—time up and nothing to show—only a hash of odd pieces of rubbish—like this." The paper ball sang through the air to the fireplace, it was so hard. "My uncle said then—" Dick checked for a moment, to get right the words of the aphorism.

"I know," Fay slipped in, with a tang of scorn that kept Dick on the stare as the other demurely supplied the quotation. "'Any man may fail once, but the man who fails twice '—was that it?"

"'—Will fail always, always.'" Before Dick well knew, the ironic gleam had leaped over to him; his voice had caught up and carried along the derisive primness of Fay's; eye to eye, the two live brains heliographed their valuation of a third brain, dead and stuffed with dead sawdust of phrasing. Then cumulus clouds of propriety piled themselves up and put out such lights.

"No doubt it's true," said the nephew, remembering. "I'm off. I'll be back in two weeks, to be sacked in form."

"Young 'un—" Fay recommenced; but it took mischief to wing words for Fay; troubled goodwill only hobbled them; he was still merely feeling his way to let fly when Dick said a deaf "Good night," and the door banged behind him.

Fay ran to it, opened it, called out: "Ah then, come back, you young fool!" the dismay in the voice hollowed to desolation; "come back, Dick! Dick!"

But Dick had the best of wax in his ears. Far away down the corridor an outer door slammed virulently. It smote like the famous conclusive bang of the door in the play, and Fay, as he turned, imagined the bite of the sound, the first term of its infinite series of bites at the mind of the husband deservedly left. Luckier he; his own wife was coming. He had reclaimed Dick's screed from the firelit tiles, smoothed the sheets, looked down them, stowed them away in the pocket you know of, and began for the first time to typewrite away with an affluent, purposeful speed, when the porter came in from the lift. Mrs. Fay was here, wishing to see him.

CHAPTER V

Ingenium velox, audacia perdita, sermo
Promptus et Isaeo torrentior. Ede, quid ilium
Esse putes? Quem vis liominem secum attulit ad nos.
JUVEKAL

The man from the lift was no slug; Mercuries-in-ordinary to these places seldom are. And Fay was no martinet either. But the man was not out of the door, to show in Mrs. Fay, when a "Quick as you can, if you please," that propelled like a kick, turned his withdrawal into a flight. Nor did Fay wait to be gnawed, sitting, by the love that feareth all things; at the first remote swish of a skirt he was up and along the passage; then back, in a moment, holding his wife by the hand, interrogating her looks with the scrutiny that fears its own satisfaction.

Mrs. Fay, from a little way off, on a windy day, might only have struck you as a working minimum of raison d'etre for so much blown cloak; nearer, you saw why the cloak was left to the enemy; all the tiny body's war was for the mastery of a vexed world of red hair; nearer still, you found among the hair a face dwarfed by it, minute and peering like a wren's, and yet valiant, and rather pretty, with a prettiness a little blurred by much work about the house and sombre thoughts on the week's bills. The cloak, and the dress it blew away from, were of a roughish cloth, not, you would say, English; they were too ill-woven and too lovely; one tear, and the cloak might rip to nothing, like a cut sweater; but it and the rest had browns, reds and russets not got from autumns or fells you see here; they were friends with the red of the hair; it and they, being together, gave and took value; and then, you might end by thinking the roughness of the stuff right too; blown about that teased, valiant speck of a face, it figured, you thought, the buffeting rudeness of the world that the mind perhaps felt itself wrapped in and beaten by. But that's rank sentiment. On.

"Is it—" Fay asked, and she seemed to know what he meant. People with only one child talk a great deal of shorthand.

"It is not. It's that newspaper office burnt down on them."

"Thank God! I made sure it was Jemmy's bronchitis." Every muscle he had went slack with relief.

"No, but the Warder—or Stalwart is it?"

"Don't you know it's the Warder you're in at this minnut?" He said "minnut." Lurking Irish slurs, cadences, idioms of his, popped out of hiding to play with hers.

"Ah, then, and how should I know, and you just as apt to be off to the one as the other?"

"An' the Stalwart's destroyed, is it? That was what took out the engines," Fay mused, with a great peace on his mind, thinking of Jemmy.

"Mr. Pinn telephoned."

"Did he own was it fire from heaven?"

"Colum!" A hand on his hair tried to steady the child that would fool at its lessons. But a grave twinkle in his eye shone on, dangerously, as she spoke. "Some stove," she said, "got too hot; that began it."

"Th' one upstairs, where they cook th' reports? Or below, for the balance sheet? Wild work they get on with at both of them."

" It's you're at the wild work, Colum. Listen." She knew he had a devil, the imp of Celtic mischief, one that will keep no close times, for the demoniac's worldly good, as do the less impracticable devils of the Teuton.

"Listen. The man beyond—Pinn—or Brumby—which is it?"

"Pinn. Brumby's the fraud in this place."

"Pinn, then—"

"Elijah Daniel Pinn." Fay gave himself up to an ecstasy of disrelish; he strung off the syllables spitefully; each might have been an emetic, mastered, but only just mastered.

"Listen now. Mr. Pinn said—to you he was speaking, the way he does always."

"Do you mean, to wan Mr. Moloney?"

"To you by that name, and I answered him for you, the way you were bidding me. He said—I have it here written." She took from her glove a half-sheet of paper. "I've told you the first part. And then he goes on—'By hook or by crook we must'"

"Crook, it'll be then," interposed the spirit of flippancy.

"'We must get out the paper to-night. I'm just going out to arrange,' I think he said, 'by God's help—.'" "He did." Fay was sure of that, though he cast some doubt, in a sceptical grunt, on the zeal of the auxiliary that Pinn had nominated.

Mrs. Fay read on, from her notes: "'—arrange for getting it printed elsewhere. Will you help by writing your—'"

"Sh!" Fay glowered round warily. "In Gath we never mention it." In the matter of motes and beams the spirit of caution is much like anyone else; Fay could go reckless drunk on the fumes of a whim of his own, and sober again at an unsafe word from another.

She read lower: "'—by writing your leader very early?'"

"Early!" Fay looked at his watch. " And it eleven-thirty now!"

She read on: "'I will send to your house for it at half-past twelve.'"

"And I here till one! A man should think what he's about before burning his office."

There was rueful silence. "What is it you do," she asked, breaking it, "other nights?"

"When they're not burnt, the one or the other?" He told her. The papers had each an idea to act on. The Warder was great on reaching the public early; the dream of the Stalwart was, more, to run up to them bursting with very late news. So the Warder was printed at two in the morning, the Stalwart, at four.

"And so—"said Fay.

The graphic ellipse was wasted on Molly. To her, what he did in the city was, one half, a matter of life and death; the other half, one of those games at which men, being all dear babies at heart, will be messing, whatever you do.

"So? " she asked.

"So a man can be here, say, from ten till one savin' away at the Empire, and then step across to the Stalwart, and save it some more—from the Warder and all such perils of the night—from a quarter past one until three, and then—"

"Then! Is it three there are?"

"There are not—yet. Not a thing for our use in the place, only these two kindly fruits of the earth. No; then the day cometh, when no man can work that's the least bit of use for a pressman." He babbled defensively, putting her off; at the bar of her mind, he could see; it went hard with his time-table.

"Colum," she broke out at last, "is it right? Two days' work every one; it's no sort of thing to be doing, and you the bad sleeper you are, a good while back."

"Well, we'll see in the morning." Word of this auroral vision was Fay's stock means of heading off whatsoever offered to corner him today. "Did the man Pinn mention a topic?"

"'The subject,'" she read on, "'of course, must be Albry's speech.'"

"There's a mor'l order"—Fay touched a bell—"there's a mor'l order in this world of ours; I can't question it, and I with the fear in my mind all the night there was nothing'd satisfy Pinn but to do the poor out of their beer, to the len'th of a column—that, or else put a stop to the church or the races or somebody's pleasure, to show that he'd not give the turn of an eye to what Albry'd be doing. If it goes on like this, I'll be coining to Mass like the man that the tree didn't fall on. Parcus deorum cultor et infrequens. Cogor relictos iter are—"

The messenger came in just as the sublimity of Fay's voice, and the other danger signal that danced in his eyes, were filling his wife with the fear of some headlong cantrip of mischief for mischief's sake. "Will you bring back that leader I sent up just now?" he said. The messenger was off for it. Fay turned again to his wife. "You'll not have heard," he said blandly, "of Sir Philip Sidney?"

"Yes, yes, but—"

"You'll see him. You'll see the leal true knight, livin' again in the Warder, rose of our modern chivalry, take from its own lips the cool, refreshing and invigoratin' leader; you'll hear it say to the poor, parched, burnin' Stalwart: ' Take it, thy need is greater than mine.'"

"Is it just the one article, Colum—and they en'mies?"

"And doesn't that make it the grand Christianity?"

"But, Colum, the Stalwart's Radical!"

"Ah, but think of their common humanity."

"Common? The Warder's that Tory you'd

"'One touch of Nature,' my dear, 'one touch of Nature.'"

She hunted for words that might bite on the slippery road of his humour. "But what'd two parties be at, to say the one thing?" was all she could find.

"Deed, what else are both for, but to say 'That's a fool there, below,' and, on great days, 'a liar'?"

"When they're just tearing, one at the other, I grant you; but to-night it's a speech that they have all the work with; and what'd the one say to that but the other'd think bad of it?"

"It's a great day when Albry speaks. Was there anything more that Pinn said?"

"There was; oh, Colum, I'm that sorry, I've forgot it."

At the little wail of remorse in her voice, his was all cooing and soothing softness. "Ah, then, wasn't it just this?—that Albry must be getting des'prate—judgin' by the len'ths he's goin'?"

She stared. "Sure, it's almost the words." Fay laughed. "Almost! He's learning variety. Did he say it was 'downright monstrous' for Albry to 'stand up charged to the muzzle with'—eh?"

"Colum, you've heard him!"

"Often. '—charged to the muzzle with statements for the absolute groundlessness of which '"—Fay's voice swung into a false gallop of banal rhetoric—"'I can imagine no other excuse than that of an ignorance truly colossal.'"

She gazed, half grasping that all it meant was that the lines of dead minds, like those of dead bodies, are rigid. And now the messenger was back, unrolling a tight cylindrical plug of paper.

"Your leader, sir." He gave it to Fay.

"Had they begun to set it?" Fay asked rather sharply.

"No, sir. Only just gone up the tube." From part to part of a newspaper office the written word, done up into cartridges, is blown or sucked along pneumatic pipes which illuminate the principles of air-guns. Fay, the messenger gone, smoothed out the typewritten sheets. His wife was to carry them home in her hansom, now waiting, and have them ready for the Stalwart's messenger. "You're uneasy, Molly?" he said; he still saw a misgiving.

"Colum," the damned-up misgivings broke out again, "it can't be it'll read the right way in the Stalwart, and it written every word for the Warder, and you not changing a tittle?"

"Listen, dear unbeliever. Will you stop me the first word that's wrong?" With the precious seconds tricking away, he set off to read the leader aloud, slowly, in deprecatory tones.

"'With Lord Albry's speech of last night the question of the hour enters on a new phase.'"

She demurred. " And so Mr. Pinn thinks these great things of Lord Albry's speech!"

"As an instance of public depravity? Surely."

Fay pleaded with sweet reasonableness. As he read on, he worked up to a ponderous gusto of delivery, faithfully placing a vapid reader's zestful stress on whatever was most hackneyed in the worn turns of phrase and the trite, switch-back curves of the rhythm.

"'Is it not time to come back to the facts? After all, it is they alone that matter. We cannot, indeed, affect to believe that in plainly stating these facts we shall carry with us all of those who have shown such deplorable proneness to blink them.'"

"There now! You see how the Liberals catch it!" she interjected.

"Liberals?" Fay looked down the sheet with the ironic care of Shylock searching for the mention of a surgeon. "I cannot find it; 'tis not in the bond."

"Why isn't it, then, and that meant for the Warder?"

"Truth is, I'd the thought in my head that no one would mind if you took it for granted it wasn't himself was the ass." He read on:

" 'On their motives, at least on the motives with which they set out, we cast no imputation.'"

"There's nothing in this world," Fay annotated, "to equal charity, for dressing down the wicked." He continued:

"'In the first instance, no doubt, they were moved by a genuine, though curiously misdirected, wish to serve the public. It might even be hard to say at what point they were first assailed by an uneasy sense of having blundered and of having been exposed. We have by us no instrument of moral mensuration with which to define the precise proportions of self-deception and of wilful misrepresentation in the case that they now lay before the public. It has always till now been a rule of English public life that men endeavouring to shape momentous public decisions—'"

"This'll be Albry, now, mind you," Fay inter-posed, and went on:

"'—should maintain some sort of relation between their public statements or pledges and the actual or potential facts. Is all this to be now changed? No doubt the conditions of public life have been, in many ways, so much altered—'"

"In the Stalwart," was Fay's parenthetic note, "that'll do for a wipe at any young blackguards they've broke for playin' the beast in the Guards, and turned out to do it in Parliament. In the Warder it's one for these Labour members, and others that's nearly as bad, they and their bowler hats, with a black tail coat, destroyin' all before them." He proceeded:

"'—so much altered that it might be sanguine to expect conformity to quite the most exacting standards of controversial accuracy, clearness, and courtesy. Still, we must warn those who have trespassed so far on public forbearance, that there is a point past which no country will lightly permit those who seek its suffrages to go. That point has been reached, if not passed. Already the offenders' conduct has sensibly lowered the standard of responsibility in English public life, as surely as it has marred the tone of English public discussion. Of that offence the community will undoubtedly take note; and our people, if slow to judge in cases like this, are also firm in the duty of punishment. We hold the strongest opinion that nothing but early and full repentance and amendment can now save the culprits from a lesson that will last them for a generation.'"

"There!" said Fay in a rhadamanthine tone of austerity, in keeping with the text. "End of first paragraph."

"Aye, but who's to know what all the bother's about?" objected the lady. You see, she had too much to do in the house to keep up with the progress of style in our daily polemics.

Fay was impressively shocked at her failure. "Not def'nite, amn't I? Just hear, now. The second paragraph begins." He read on incisively:

"'We are forced to state the point at issue in this somewhat plain and bald fashion '—You see how def'nite I am!—' because there has grown up so noticeable an aversion to the cold touch of realities in the minds of those who know only too well how soon a plain tale would set them down.'"

He gave her a look, as of apology for an excess of brutal directness. "We're forced, as you see, to be def'nite, we virile Conservative—what's that I'm saying?—we clear-sighted guides of Lib'ral opinion." He recommenced reading, severely:

"'In words, like weeds, they wrap them o'er,
Like coarsest cloak against the—'"

"Colum!" the tiny woman almost shouted.

"'Like coarsest cloak,'" he went on, a little nervously, as though there were something he hoped might blow past, "'against the cold.'"

"Colum, what mad work are you at? I thought I knew every word that you read; now that verse reminds me. Why, wasn't it I looked it up in the bookcase, to see was it ' coarsest ' or ' roughest,' and you writing all that leader at home, a good year back?"

"The first sentence, is it, I wrote a good year back?—'with Lord Albry's speech of last night the question of the hour '—'of the hour'—mind you. Be just now. Warm from the mint, and that's what it is."

"Aye, but the rest—the whole full of the column?"

He shrugged. He was loftily concessive. "In a sense, I'll allow—in a certain limited sense you're entitled to say it was written about all the work that there was last year with the firm that mis-built the main drain. But be fair. It wasn't printed. Some bad Emp'ror died that night, and had to be kicked in the coffin; what with that and one thing and another, no soul but the two of us saw it from that day to this. An' now shall the innocent perish, blighted for ever by th' accident that marred its birth? Never. Let bygones be bygones. One aspect, I grant you, one superficial, one technical aspect of the issue has since then been modified. But fundamentally? No. There's entirely too much made of details in discussin' these broad public questions that go to th' roots of our common nature, when—isn't the gist of the matter the same in each wan?—that th' other side hasn't the stim of a pipe for a leg to stand up on."

His accent was always enriched when the elf in him rollicked; here, when constrained to keep other expression demure, that gnome would take its indemnity. She did not give combat—merely considered the doctrine silently, with a literal mind's bewilderment. He looked at his watch. "Twelve ten, be Zeus!" While he folded the leader for her to take, she came behind him and stroked his hair. "And you'll be staying here, working," she said with a whole motherhood's ache of love and pity in the hang on the last word. His head rose to the stroke like a cat's; it pressed up to feel the hand's kindness. He spoke lightly, with the pleasure of it on him.

"I'll just rig up a something for Brumby, now this one's been lost on him—what is it, Molly?" The soothing hand had stopped dead.

"What's that you have there?" she asked, pointing down among the papers on the desk. He was embarrassed.

"It's it," he owned. Three days ago, descanting one holiday night on the ways of the musical critics he knew in the city, Fay had said that a notice as written by any of them would apply just as well, and no better, to any one concert than to any other; more—he had spouted, by way of illustration, while she typewrote it, a typical, universal concert-notice, true of all concerts past, present and to be, with unprejudiced blanks duly left for the names of any performers whatever. There it was, now, half out from under his blotter.

"You're using it?" she asked in horror. She knew he had drifted of late into odd jobs of writing on music.

"As a concert-notice, seriously? Oh, no." " Don't ask me," the virtuous voice seemed to say, "to plead to a charge so wild as all that." For the moment she was eased. "That," he went on in the same tone of cheerful vindication, holding the typed stuff up and nodding impressively, "that's all but a picture-notice by now." He paused, to taste the effect, while she dropped into a chair with a remonstrant gesture of cluelessness in the maze of his freaks. Again he was sweetly reasonable.

"Think! Aren't the arts one, really? Did you ever see anny but just the wan book of life, and them all at it, tearin' out pages?"

"Pooh!" said his wife. She thought of the hansom, waiting, earning its half-crown per hour. "What!" There remained to him irony, last resource of the thinker in an unthinking world. I'll engage there's no ars artium either! No tract of vast truths common to all these strivin', isolated arts! No greatest common measure, shall I say, of—"

It was too maddening, with the minutes—each, perhaps, a future pound to the house of Fay, each a present halfpenny, beyond doubt, to the cabman—trickling, ticking, away.

"Colum," she cried, distressed, "will you quit public speakin' and say what you're at?"

At the note of distress he came right off his high horse, to be with her, comrade with comrade, all the play put aside. "Listen now, Molly. There's a boy here they've corralled; the jungle look isn't out of him yet; if you saw his eyes, the way they're big and shiny with all the good-faith he has ragin' inside him! On trial he is, at doin' odd jobs, an' to-day he was sent off to see some pics; an', God help him, the pics went straight to his head, till he saw—th' intoxicated creature saw—just what the men were about that had painted them. Fact is, he's a child"—Mrs. Fay, now absorbed, gave an audible purr—"he's not been kicked out of the Kingdom of Heaven—not properly—yet. So in he shankin', full from the feast, eyes shinin'"—Fay had not seen, but he knew—"and sits down to typewrite the visions he's had; good stuff it was too—I've the full of a breast pocket here—only no decent paper'd be turnin' truth naked out into the streets, while there's sawdust and bran left to pack her away in. He knew it; the groans he let out of him bet all that ever I heard, till, 'Here's out of it,' he says at last, fit to leap down your throat if you'd stand in the way, and he quitted; no holdin' him. Done for, that's what he said he was." Fay paused. Compassion tormented her visibly. Fay fed it at intervals. "I've a fear for his post," he would say, and then wait while it worked; and then again: "Brumby's own nephew—I'd not trust the man, but he'd offer to play Roman uncle, he's that wild to be at the posin'."

"Colum," she said at last shamefacedly, "could you—do anything?"

"Did you think"—he deftly transferred the initiative—"did you think any good could be done with that notice of ours—the one of the concert? Was it starting it fresh, with just the few lines we've the time for, you thought of? And curling a tail to the end of it? Not a doubt but it might save the post for him." She kissed his hair, grateful for the scheme. "Ah, but you're the wicked woman, to dream of it," he said, delighted. "Will you help me, now?"

"Darling!" She made a gesture of readiness.

They fell to work, with his watch on the table to keep them hurrying. He gave her the concert notice, a goodish bundle. "Just the one temp'-rate judgment on each page," he said. Then he took up the catalogue. "Personalities, so far, eschewed; but in this I'll engage I'll find some one'll not be the worse for whatever's on each page we come to." She, at the typewriter was to read out each page; he, raking the catalogue, was to fit praise or blame with a meet object; she would then type the chosen name into the blank space awaiting it. They worked, grim and intent, talking low, like hurried and sobered children. She ran through, to begin with, "some words" as he said, "to step up to the genuine theme, I was just after writing the moment you came." They were:

"'Halland's Fifteenth Winter Exhibition—this time of Mountain Paintings—may fairly be said to be marked, on the whole, by a higher average level of achievement than the corresponding exhibitions of the past few years. Sir Joshua's cardinal precept that Art must "see large" has clearly been taken more closely to heart by the best of our younger men. We may make our meaning more clear if we pass at once to the work of a few of the most salient contributors.'"

Reaching across to the pile of remaining slips, he took off the top half. "We'll cut the cards first," he said;

"we'll be fair to the creatures, and they not here." He put the top half at the bottom. "Will you deal now?"

She read the top page:

"'Mr.—has a talent—we use the word advisedly—to which it is only too easy to do less than justice. He may, as some think, have not yet compassed the whole ascent from the mood of graceful prose to that of serene and elevated poetic feeling. But at least it is something to have the ground clear and unquestionably fertile, for the seeds of future breadth and resolution.'"

"That'd harm nobody breathin'," said Fay, as she stopped. "Give it to Portland—F. Portland. They say he's sold nothing this twelvemonth."

"P-o-r-t-l-a-n-d." She dropped the word into its niche, then took up the next page and read:
"' The always sound and competent work of—'"

"Ah, then, write in' Mrs. Henleigh,'" he interrupted, on catching the eulogy; "if you saw how he's drinkin', that husband she has! He's goin' beyond the beyonds. But p'rhaps we'll read on first." She continued:

"'—reminds us that some fairly authoritative judges have perhaps dissociated the work of the older school '"

"Eh?" he had a misgiving.

"'—from that of their ablest latter-day followers more widely than strict chronology warrants.'"
Fay was pensive. "There's no doubt it's a delicate thing, that, to say of a lady."

"And she that irritable!" Molly added. "Pass a single remark—that she doesn't look well, or no matter what, and God help you. It's a poor thing to be sensitive."

"Aye, we'll keep on the safe side. 'John Rome,' then. We'll see to her later."

Mr. Rome got his ration. "Ah, but here's the sweet one," she said, taking up the next page.

"Whetlien, make it Mrs. Henleigh and have done with it." He eyed the watch anxiously." Just rush through, d'you think—case of accident?"

She gabbled with haste; commas vanished, full stops shrank to commas; it all had a pleasing effect on the judgmatical style.

"'What shall we say of—Mrs. Henleigh? No one is more thoroughly aware than he that—'"

"'She,'" said Fay. "Lucky we looked." His wife made an "s" with a pen, and went on:

"'—she that in art it is as fatal to push simplicity to the point of shallowness—we do not say infanticism—as it is to seek to dazzle the public with the insolence of a workmanship which obtrudes its own triumphs over difficulties raised only to be overcome; everything more-over that this artist does proclaims its authorship. That in itself is much, the only question is whether his—her—work—'"

While listening, Fay took out some papers. "'Scuse me," he said, while she stopped to reverse the gender. "I'll be sortin' out th' outward semblance of a column upon Albry for the Warder, in lieu of what you have on you. It's the good half-hour's work, trimming it down, and the night near through." "Darling, of course." While she read on, she knew he was minding, even in the act of seeing to it that the Warder's clarion note should not fail at the dawn.

"'—whether her work does not actually over-represent, if we may use the phrase, her natural powers. Meanwhile h—she has at any rate the qualities of—her—defects. It is no wonder the French love—her.'"

"We'll take that out," said Fay, " about the French. You know what Henleigh is."

She deleted; then she took up the next page.

"'. . . has evidently gone to head-quarters for her technique.'"

"'Her ' this time?" said Fay, scanning the catalogue. "Say 'Miss Wincot.' Saves so much correcting. Yes? We'll just see what it is."

"'So far, too, as her work is in any sense individual, it goes to confirm the standing she has already acquired.'"

"Right. Next."

She read:

"'We do not envy those who would deny to Mr. — the germ, at any rate, of force, fire, thought, imagination, or the power to pick his way between the Scylla of a flimsy and pyrotechnic handling of his material and the Charybdis of a sombre and morose elaboration of profundity.'"

He did not speak at first when she stopped. She looked up. "Old Thomason, d'you think?" he said hesitatingly.

"It is a nice one," she said longingly; "but perhaps we'd do right not to give it to him that's our friend."

"No," he sighed. It was a bitter sacrifice to critical integrity. His voice ran over the catalogue's index of names—"Bence, Bonus, Credland, Curtayne."

"Curtayne?" She stopped him. "He'll be Irish."

"Aye, is he," said Fay; "from the County Roscommon. Shall we?"

"Yes," she said, with decision, and clicked in the name.

"Do you think," said Fay, looking again at the watch, "you would look out for Thomason one we could give him in reason and he none the worse? There's a slating or two, in the bundle you have there, would not hurt a fly, and he'd liefer be slated than have nothing said of him, good, bad, or middling."

"Will this do?" she asked, after a scrutiny:

"'Mr.— has, we are aware, been highly praised by those who know. But what, we would ask, are the qualities of an artist of the first rank? Surely dignity, reticence, ordered spontaneity; nerve in the best sense—the sense of a robust felicity that goes directly, almost brusquely, to the heart of the matter in hand—largeness and simplicity of conception; a sane and lofty positiveness, as it were, of execution; rigour to discipline the unessential; a plastic power not necessarily carried to sculpturesque extremes of cold and austere abstraction—but need we go on? That Mr.—has some, nay, most of these attributes, no one could deny. But has he them all?'"

"Well, since we must slate him," said Fay. She put in the name. "That'll near do us," he said, an anxious eye on the watch. "Perhaps just another."

She read: "'At this concert—'"

"Concert how are you?" He came with a full pen and blotted out every letter of the indiscretion. She read out the amended text:

"'In this fairly representative exhibition we are once more reminded, by the personal and vital work of Mr. —, of a speculation that has no doubt occupied many besides ourselves. Is it, one asks oneself, a very rule of Nature, after all, that the complete and rounded development of a true artist should invariably exhibit a second, or intermediate period, marked mainly by a buoyant sympathy with outward things, midway between the usual first period, with its delicate finish of execution and versatility of fancy, and the third period, with its masterfully sure and speedy grasp, its intense realization of one leading aspect of the subject, on the other?'"
"Half the rest might toss for that," said Fay thoughtfully, thumbing the catalogue over. "Oh, there's Thorold has nothing yet. T-h-o-r-o-l-d."

She put it in. "I'll gum a tail to it," he said, pocketing the unappropriated residue of valuations. She understood and sat ready to type. He dictated, ten or twelve words at a time, working at the Warder's leader while the typewriter overtook each lead of the voice, but never missing his thread, nor, it would seem, undergoing more mental strain than if he were whistling.

"'The show as a whole is certainly some degrees richer than such shows often are in the elements of passion and sheer primal force, though cases will occur to every one in which these qualities verge dangerously on sentimentalism and melodrama. Possibly it also includes fewer of those obvious arrangements of checks and balances which may engage and satisfy the intellect, but leave the heart cold.'"

He paused an instant, musing. "You see what it wants now is a technical tag. Turned on to pics, the best concert notice you'll find in general." He sighed. "Fact is—what you need unless you're a real art critic, is seein' th' actual show. Thry this." He dictated again:

"'Some luck there may be of what we would call architectural power, the faculty of laying out on a great scale; but against that we must set an unmistakeable advance—'"

They're getting on you know," he put in for himself. "Why, what's to stop them?" He went on:

"'—advance in the nice economy of artistic means and in solidity and confidence in the actual use of paint.'"

He released a breath of relief. "We're over the water. Nothin', only a straight run in, before us now."

The dictation flowed out of him.

"'We have far from exhausted this show's merits, or, indeed, its defects. But we cannot close without a word in recognition of a certain note of mellow and brooding thoughtfulness, a tender lustre almost Vergilian in its sad sunshine. Many may overlook it, but to our mind it gives a savour of its own to this year's work of some of the men who really count.'"

"They've a great way, I notice," he said, as she typed the last words, "of nailin' all down with one last slam of gen'rous int'mate appreciation."

The session ended in a scramble. Fay pressed a bell, took the sheets from her, initialled the top one, "To show I've run through the boy's work," marked the heading for "Pica," the text "bgs," and gave the whole to the messenger, by this time at his elbow.

"Has Mr. Brumby come in?" Fay asked.

"Comin' upstairs, sir, now." The messenger went. Mrs. Fay looked scared. What if he found her here, on her unavowable errand?

"He'll be in by this door," said Fay, opening one of the many; no step sounded near yet. "That's ours," he showed an opposite door. "Players," he rippled on, gay now that the moment was ticklish. "Merely players—' they have their exits and their entrances.'" He fastened her cloak at the throat, peaceably fitting the hook and eye. "No time to see you into the cab, is it? In the time the horse'd be gettin' a hold of his feet I'll be reachin' down Brumby the fit of the world for the state that he's in after readin' the mountebank, Albry. I have it here now. Never fear, but I'll just get along the best way I can. You'll see in the morning."

He fairly babbled; for one savoursome moment, when all was in order for going, he still hung on, to taste the sound of Brumby's step in the passage. Such shaves were to him, in his trade, what the risk is to soldiers and hunters in theirs. Scapin, like Cyrano, wants to be helped to that spice, and the mites in the cheese may dimly feel in hours of insight that a bloom would be rubbed off life if a knife were sure not to come down at the end of the next inch they bore. Fay bored away in the cheese with a will, having three souls to bore for, and dared the beckon of doom with as much delight as Montrose or a child that is playing Tom Tiddler. The one door's handle was rattling in Brumby's hand as Fay's left the outer knob of the other. He had a shiver of pleasure, his wife one of fear, as they slipped downstairs together.

CHAPTER VI

Now, you have what is termed, descriptively, a Recognition when some one or more of the people, whose fate you are meant to see, come to know of a thing they had not known, and fall out with a friend, or make friends with a stranger. And a Recognition tells best at the very turning-point of a story. *ARISTOTLE, Poetics, Chap. XI*

Brumby came in with a seated joy in his face; some god might look so, after a day when the altars had smoked right and niggard man had for once made no bones about paying up all that he owed of fat and myrrh.

Committees for doing good are poor gadding things as a rule. To-night his had kept to the point. The chairman, in a plea for imperilled. Church Training Colleges, had brought all minds back to thoughts of the Warder—"a public, I may say, a national, institution"; the Dean, not at all the man to say smooth things, had ended by flashing one ray of hope across a sombre descant on the modern infant's slackening grasp of dogma; all was not lost, he had said, "while such morning and evening stars as the Warder and Evening Warder fought in their courses for the cause of God." Poetry, and good at that, Brumby had mused, scanning the last words in his beatitude while they were fresh: "fought in their courses for the cause of God"; good as Milton, and George Brumby was still seeing new beauty in metre when the High Sheriff moved to condole with the late Bishop's widow—a speech like a soldier's funeral, all dead march and irreparable loss till half-way through, and then an "Ad laetiora vertamur." and back at the quickstep of "Nobody's indispensable," bracing all hearts with a sense of good fish left in the sea, and loaves on shore, and competent fishers of men, the Sheriff ran on, a little confusedly, to fish the dioceses of our Galilee; aye, and spiritually-minded laymen. Some one, he thought, had mentioned a great, he said advisedly, a great journal known to them all; the Warder, they all knew, was Mr. Brumby, and Mr. Brumby the Warder; and character, individuality in the best sense, was everything, everywhere, and as for thy sting, O death, it was nowhere, absolutely nowhere; the Bishop, in short was in Heaven and all was well with the world.

So had Brumby felt too, as he walked back under the stars, with man's benediction, to say the very least, upon him. Evil itself at such times is a problem resolved; faith need no longer be shaken by phenomena like Pinn; for, as life could not be had but on terms of death, so evil must come that good might be; to beat out perfection the hammer of right must fall on an anvil of wrong; in the world there was room and work even for those who should only serve, by the foulness of their darkened minds, to call out the strength of the children of light; why, if that barren fig tree had not been there to be cursed, men might never have heard of the faith that removes mountains. How little there was, after all, to blue-pencil in all things created. Little? Nothing. Brumby, to-night, could initial the universe.

From the starry fane of a deserving Creator, Brumby passed into the hand-made temple dedicated to himself. Good outside, it was better still to be here. Round him all the hive buzzed and hummed, as he dropped into his chair, luxuriating; in the cellar the big machines were fidgeting for the start, their signal bells, tinkling now and again, might have been on the ears of impatient horses; the murmur from the readers' room had gained speed, while keeping its quality of carefulness, as a good crew will quicken the stroke up to anything asked, and still, within each beat of the boat's speeded pulse, keep, contained and unhurried, one fractional movement of rhythmical leisure; the messengers, who had walked, now ran; every limb of the huge thing, as of one horse, had gathered pace together, in a consummate unity, the unity of being he; yes, the Sheriff was right—it was all an expression of him, an extension of him, a flowering forth of his strength, his rich nature, his sense as a man of the world, his warmth as a good fellow; if something could come at that moment to try him he'd let people know. Like a man as yet only the better for liquor, he basked in the warm, shining reverie. If only something would come! And it did. Pat as the right man turns up in a play, there came up the lift the card of "Mr. Elijah D. Pinn."

"Gentleman wishes to see you, sir," said the porter, thrilled. He knew who was who, did the porter. Brumby leapt straight out of reverie into gifted action. The porter was ordered to put Mr. Pinn in the library, leave him exactly five minutes, and then show him in. That much cooling of heels would be good for the man; more would be rude. And one wants just to give a look round, and have things as they should be, before speaking with an enemy in the gate. Brumby tidied the gate. He put on the table four letters he had for the post, with the one to a peer on top; he whipped out of sight the memoir, in proof, of a Halland big-wig whom Pinn, with luck, might not know to be dying. He lit a cigar, to put down when Pinn should come in; he did not know Pinn, but the bloodless stick—Brumby's heart told him—was sure not to smoke, and the smell would make him feel out of it.

Three of the five minutes fleeted by in these hospitable cares; it was time to take ground on the hearth rug, securely based on the fire; the adversary was to have his face raked by the big hanging light— Brumby thoughtfully fixed the site of the chair he would offer; then, on a knock at the door he leapt back to his base. No! only Fay, to report on his vicegerency.

"Come in, my dear fellow, come in." Brumby's geniality was exuberant above itself. Had Dick's notice gone upstairs?

"You'll see a proof in ten minutes," said Fay; did no higher interest forbid he seldom grudged truth the homage of equivocation.

"He'll do yet, that boy," said the uncle. "Not too individual, I hope? These young critics are so very individual sometimes."

"I don't think you'll find it excessively so. But you'll see," said Fay moderately.

"Good. Your leader up, too?"

"Not all of it—sorry to say." Not a word was up really; but why put things crudely? "Ten minute's more'll do me. I'll be off and end up in my room. Shall I look in, last thing?"

"Do, my dear fellow. Don't let me keep you." Fay went, with his typewriter. At one point in the corridor there was nothing between him and Pinn but three feet of air and the opacity of a pane of corrugated glass. Another two minutes, and almost half of the Warder's new leader was blown up the tube, to be set, and Brumby was taking a first look at Pinn.

Brumby had dreamt of such a man. Conservatives have. Pinn was a Tory nightmare come true; in a made-up tale, you would say he was too purely a type to be an individual—that, except in thought, there could be no one lean man so juiceless, so literal, so bitten with an itch for posting, eyes front, across wastes of sand and thorns to Gileads that he could not see and that he would not really like. There have always been Pinns, or at least approaches to Pinns, attempts at being Pinn; "Forty years endured I their manners in the wilderness"—you see the rudimentary Pinns of Israel, round the camp-fire of a night, grumbling at manna and quails, hating the man who laughs, who sleeps easy, who sings a good song, when we ought to be getting on, on, as we should be, too, if Moses were straight. Ours, the ultimate Pinn, Nature's finished piece of the kind, was all for reform of course, but as one whom reform could never leave musing at last, in a world put to rights, "Behold, it is good"; when he talked retrenchment, it sounded so hollow, you could not tell why till you tried to figure him spending a coin, with the joy of a boy, on any known product of earth; he cried, "Peace, Peace," and to every man quiet under his fig tree, and you looked and thought, "What a man to sit with, under a fig tree!" and you felt that peace hath her horrors no less to be dreaded than war's. All life, for him, was a taking of means to ends; means that to him had no worth but as ways to their ends; ends that were nothing but termini for means, means he could not smell as flowers, to ends he could not taste as fruit. Imagine his coming distress in Paradise, the fretting of the irrigator out of work, called from the Saharas of his choice to wander through Elysian fields watered with honeyed dews. And yet—if he gets there first you may find a pure-air movement humming in the largior aether, and Pinn, torn to pieces with work, three meetings a day, reforming sourly the housing of the saints.

Brumby had thought that he knew all this. The stock Tory does know it. Heir to the Cavaliers' spites, he knows how to debit the stock Radical with all his Roundhead father's indisposition for joy. But to see Pinn in the flesh—the little flesh that he had—was for Brumby to know what knowing meant. All very well—it seemed now—to have let fly, blind, at the hosts of Gath; here was another affair, the very sight of his own arrow billeted, plump and fairly, in the carcase of a standard Philistine. All the strained, cold lines bitten into Pinn's face by the taking of corrosive thought swore to the rightness of that picture drawn at a venture; loveless philanthropy glowered out of the exacting servant of mankind; the thistle seemed only the more of a thistle for striving to bear the grapes for which it was not designed. No one more bitterly set on doing "the masses" good; no one more unimaginable smoking a pipe on a bench in the sun for a talk, for talk's sake, with a basking tramp, or to see the lusty black babies roll in the grass. Brumby's flesh crawled like a horses's at smelling a camel.

To Brumby the abstract was naught, mere principles dross, a major premise the crackling of thorns. Right intuitive action—that was the thing; good-natured impulse more than morality; not the Commandments—their letter, I mean; that killeth; rather, a gentleman's perception, the free spirit which—in a sense, quite rightly—they sought to pin down into forms. Politics, no more than conduct, was the mass of prude's syllogisms that the Pinns of this world would make them; better keep them simply branches of the art of extemporizing ever and ever, o'er and o'er, from the wealth of your own nature, earth's noblest spectacles, a "decent human being," and a "sensible man of the world." Shame on the pettifogger who fussed about "rights" of his own or anyone else's, or let his spirit take cold with hanging about, looking before and after, when "problems" arose. Problems!—as if there were any, while you play the man, as he might fairly say he had done—for recollection was a gallery of portraits—Alexander, Brennus, Nelson, all of them himself, cutting Gordian knots, throwing swords into scales, standing with telescopes to blind eyes, improvised ones if need be, doing every prodigy of gumption that ever struck clayey souls all of a heap. And beyond the still, strong men, the risers to crises, the hitters of nails on their heads, there was the happy virilist in his hours of ease, genial as summer; not perfect—who is?—not a bad fellow, though, after all.

See the mellowed, jocund English look; it took you to yellowing Gloucester orchards and jolly brown faces in the brown corn.

A virtue, they say—courage or liberality—should not be used up in the mere act of standing fire or giving away; it should work in us always, warming us, lighting us up. Brumby's love for the one dear image was of that quality; no time but he felt the better for it; no day could choke with its petty dust a soul so regularly flushed out with a full, flooding sense of itself in all its own easy riches, its rollicking invincibility, dominating circumstance. As he stood ravished before that picture, nay, almost knelt, as it were in an oratory, the ideal reaffirmed its claims; yes, by George, to his own self he would be true; or, rather, from strength to strength go on; like a boy in bed at night, who will make that great drive to the on again to-morrow, just the same, only harder, so would he bend up every fibre of him to exist as he was, but intensified, redoubled.

We are told that if love must first fill a pool, it will hardly water the ground; his to-night was so great, it brimmed over; it sought things to be good to; it would not stick at vermin even; let them lap. So the meeting was, on his side, cordial; civil, of course, it had to be; to the outer world it would be a call of cat upon dog; the mere thought of that put biting and scratching out of the question. Sapless Cassius and juicy humanist had to pretend to a certain community of flesh and blood. But Brumby, in his glory, paid no bare dues. Benignly he shook hands; benignly he planted Pinn in the armchair; benignly, after the first salutation, he looked down from his six feet of height to hear what sounds this scorpion would make who, like us, was God's creature.

"You have every right," said Pinn, "to feel surprised."

"Oh, no!" Brumby courteously renounced the privilege. He was charmed, only.

"I mean, we've not met, I think, ever," said Pinn, feeling his way towards business.

"Well, no." Brumby was lifted above earth, but not quite so high that the tone of this could be purely benignant. Met, indeed! Was anyone likely to meet this charmless, cantankerous prude, with his beard like the sum of a series of hairy moles, among Brumby's friends, five-meal, meat-fed, tweed-clad men with red necks and neat white moustaches, whose place, you could see at a glance, was the cover side, men who warmed both hands at the fire of life, rode and shot straight, and talked—well, as men that are men do talk in their hours of ease, and felt that woman would lose her poetry should she ape man and take to affairs.

"Except in print," Pinn fumbled about for an opening, "and there—" He paused, but was not helped out. It is easy waiting on a hearth-nag. So Pinn gave it up, cast back, and made a fresh start, abruptly, with a grim plainness, "Mr. Brumby, you hit pretty hard."

"I?"

"You. The Warder. It's the same thing."

"You feel that?" said Brumby softly; it pleased him so.

"Who should, if not I?"

"Oh, we don't take things so hard as that," Brumby purred. It was good to see Pinn rub his wounds.

"What was it yesterday?" Pinn half-soliloquized, hugging the shaft that stuck in him, "'a compost of maudlin sentiment and gabbling abuse.'"

Brumby listened, leaning out over the bar of heaven. "War's war, you know," he murmured sweetly. What a wrist that beggar, Fay, had! What a God's mercy to have him!

Pinn had not done. "Yesterday—'Pragmatical pedants complicated with a touch of the poltroon.'"

"War, you know, war." Who is the happy warrior if not he to whom it is given to see his own soft-nosed bullet meet the bone, expand and shatter and lacerate?

"Last week—'sophists labouring to plunge others in their own moral slough.'"

"War, my dear sir. Can't do it in kid gloves, you know." The target had done so well, in its station in life, that the good-natured marksman would tell it the right way to shoot.

That was a little too much. "Oh, yes, I know," said Pinn, sombrely dispensing with tuition in his trade; "I don't dispute the power of the writing. The world allows you brilliancy." Brilliancy might have been harlotry's diamonds, the note was so acrid. "Still—why make any bones about it?—it is I that am struck—by you."

You know how experts spit; the words were emitted with that jet, that patness. The last went at Brumby's face with a momentum that startled him out of a complacent reverie on his choice of Fay. "Me!" he said, still half absent.

"Is it not you?" The pace at which this discharge left the muzzle, the way each word was its own bullet self, and yet all, like a good charge of pellets, kept together in the air, were the last word in the technics of expectoration.

Brumby spoke with the quiet, kindly dignity granted by Nature to the holder of the upper hand. "I admit the pen may be mine; I don't say it isn't; but remember I'm only a man, as you are; only a—well, I hate talking about these things, but a—tool in the hand of something else, something rather bigger than I." It was pretty to hear the strong man, modest even about being modest, playfully make light of his humility. "Now don't you see? It's a cause that writes; not I; a cause."

"Through you, at me." Suppliant though he was, Pinn would stand in at no debauches of flummery. He had not the time. Setting as much of his face as was not hard set already, he went the big jump.

"Through you, at me. Well, I've come to say 'I'm in your power; here's the "sophist"; you've got him; stop the "pedant"—you can if you wish; it's for you to say whether the "compost" shall come out tomorrow, or, possibly, never come out again.' The Stalwart was burned out an hour ago."

At each fresh snort that he gave, as he quoted the other's picked gems of ribaldry, Finn felt he had blasted his own mission anew. He did not care, now. He was past caring. It had been a clear duty to come; a syllogism had ordered it. Major premise: he was morally bound to leave nothing undone to save the public the calamity of a blank, Stalwart-less dawn. Minor premise: the Warder alone, in all Hal land or anywhere near, had the plant left to bring out the Stalwart tonight. Conclusion: he had to ask Brumby to do it. But the fury of mortification in Pinn had taken a savage satisfaction in bating no jot of acidity; Brumby should have the case to put him stark and bald—no grovelling or wheedling. So we rough-hew our ends, and the divinity shaping them had so played on Brumby to-night that no other tone could have answered so well. Tuned right up to the heroic pitch, all he could wish was that chivalry's demands on him should be handsome; the harder the thing he was asked to do, the better; the less grace in the asking, the finer the rapture in giving.

Still, he was, as he had said, but a man; and this was the first he had heard of the fire. The news was tremendous; the mind needed a moment to bite on it. When first Hamlet heard of the ghost, he paid out idle little queries to keep his informants in play, held off at arm's length, till he grasped the new state of things in its hugeness. So too, Brumby.

"You can't print?" he asked, knowing quite well.

"The plant's a scrap-heap, red-hot."

"Well?" said Brumby mechanically. "Well?" He knew what must come; he was not racking Pinn from ill-will; he was only taking a hold.

"Well, it's my duty to ask, will you print us to-night, here?" The tooth was out, anyhow, now—so Pinn felt as he ended; the hog would refuse, and this hell would be done with.

"Ah!" said Brumby slowly. He had a hold now; he saw the way; only, he must have time; first, to set in a right line, in both their minds, the metal he was made of, metal now to come out; then, too, to do justice to a certain quick new impulse born of his nice sense of form in the bearing of man to man; for in saying those last words Pinn had mystically changed; he had begged; however ill-done, it was begging; knightliness, carried far, might deliver him out of the fire, to be spitted, in due time, on the knightly deliverer's sword, these being the duties in life to which each was called; still, Pinn had begged; caste was gone from him; Brumby's instinct for manner had built in an instant a lobby of silence, of expectation, for beggars to wait in; if only ten seconds.

Pinn fidgeted in it. "Of course there is no mechanical difficulty." He only said it because to say nothing was like sitting down in the hall, with his hat on the floor, while his prayer was looked through in the parlour.

"I'm not so sure," said Brumby, remote and occupied. "Still," he went on, as if communing with some one apart, on the waiting suppliant's fate, "we'll waive that. In itself it would not be fatal."

"I know, I know," said Pinn, in his torment, struggling again to the parlour-door that closed in his face; "it's the moral effort. I know." He rose. There was no sitting down under this. He was pointed back to his chair.

"Please," Brumby said. But the long wait was over; on Brumby's face the glory of a noble climax was now coming up like a dawn.

"Mr. Pinn, I'm a very plain man, and I'll say to you plainly, you do ask much; and you're right—no one knows how much better than you, for you know what you've written—may I say what you've personally written?" Pinn nodded darkly—a statue of stern veracity swearing to its own hurt. Brumby bowed—"What you've personally written now for many years, particularly"—a spasm of wrathful recollection shook Brumby and was gone—"in the last few years. Well, you say it rests with me whether that sort of thing shall go on or stop—for a day, perhaps altogether. My answer is this: I wouldn't lift a hand, I wouldn't stir an inch, to save your paper if—" He really could not forgo a second's pause. Why have such moments at all, if you are not to taste them?

Pinn rose, tragic. "I have done my duty," he said; it was thus, always, he said he had failed.

But Brumby's moral grandeur was striding on over the break. "—if you hadn't come like this and put it to me straight that I had got this fist home on you and that you felt the weight of it." And thereat Brumby presented the fist to Pinn; first clenched for purposes of recognition, then opened cordially.

"Sir," he said in a transport of appreciation of the way the thing was coming off," you're a cursed Puritan, but you're a man. Weill print you to the—well, the last drop of our ink." He laughed, happy in his part, happy in his wit, happy in the generosity with which it abated for Pinn the emotional strain of a crushing obligation. To the salvaged Pinn, Pinn that had been dead, now re-begotten by him, his tone was almost a father's. Pinn must just be off and make his arrangements. Or, better still, make them from there, by telephone; at the Stalwart, it seemed, there was some detached piece of the office unburnt, where the staff were now huddled. Brumby showed Pinn the instrument, fixed to the open wall of the room, and himself, sitting down, wrote a circular note to the heads of his own departments to warn them what was to come. The feel of the many reins in one hand was so good that he half forgot Pinn's own presence till a prefatory clearing of the throat re-announced it.

Pinn was fidgeting before the telephone. He rang, gave the number he wanted, and then, while waiting, he turned. "Mr. Brumby," he said with straining unconcern, "I am about to telephone an order

"One?" Brumby roared. "Is that all?"

"—an order I wish you to hear." This was not just a fib; Pinn's first dismay at sight of the open telephone not ten feet from Brumby's ear had really sunk into a sombre acquiescence in unavoidable evil which was fairly confusible with the faintly optative mood of gloom that he called wishing. The bell rang. Was that the Stalwart, Pinn asked, and then he said, "Wait!" It was clearly the Stalwart; the tone was the one to use where you know you can say to one man, "Come," and he cometh; to another man, " Go," and he goeth; to a third man, "Stand and wait," and he, also, serveth. Pinn turned again. "Let me make myself clear. I have a habit—perhaps you would call it a hobby—God knows, it may be a foible—of thinking it a duty, a peremptory duty to speak with my own voice in my own paper."

Brumby smiled. "If you're wrong to think that, I fear I can't afford to throw the first stone." "Ah! We are at one, then, there at any rate. We give our best; we give ourselves. What it costs—but there—you know."

"It takes a man, certainly," Brumby was modestly forced to own.

"Hardest of all, for men of that fibre, when forced away for an instant from the post of duty, to see their work botched, ruined perhaps by some weak or stupid substitute—it may be at some supreme, critical moment." He opened his hands melancholily; a sense of loss, loss to the individual, loss to the race, filled him. But the bell rang again; Pinn got to business. His staff were at once to migrate, bearing with them all the rescued "copy," to the Warder. Brumby listened happily. The benevolent familiarity of a conscious saviour spared him misgivings about Pinn's privacy. And then Pinn, half turning, gave him a look and "This," the look said, "is what you're to take the right way," and the next words into the telephone were: "Has Mr. Moloney's leader come in?"

"Moloney? Never heard of him," Brumby mused.

"Yes," Pinn was saying at the telephone, a messenger was to bring it from Mr. Moloney's house. "Yes. Ring me up again in three minutes and let me know. Yes. The Warier Office. Yes." Pinn left the machine.

"Moloney? I don't seem to know your man's name," said Brumby lightly, just to make talk, as these Titans of energy do when a spate of work is upon them.

You scarcely would," Pinn said. "The man is hardly a journalist of moment, in any sense."

Pinn should not have looked so unconcerned. Unconcern, on his face, caught the eye, it seemed so far out of its place. Brumby stared. Curiosity rose in him. "Was it," he said, a fierce gleam coming into his eyes, "was it—you don't mind my asking?"

"Not at all," said Pinn, much though he did.

"Was it this man Moloney that wrote your leader on Monday?"

~ Monday—let me see." Memory feigned a sort of head-scratching. Some questions one puts off answering, as one puts off paying bills, without real hope of escaping at last.

Brumby could not be put off. A sore place was itching. "I mean," he went on, with a gathering rage of irony, "the nice, kind, Christian, gentlemanly thing about us—us Jingoes, is that the word?—'sowing the fair domains of peace with dragons' teeth.' Hauling the Bible in, that way! And what's this he called the reverence some of us venture to have for our country's past?—'Chinese torpor,' was it? Why 'Chinese,' I wonder? And 'torpor'! Torpor! I suppose it's some new kind of English. Mr. Pinn, now that I've seen you, I do you the justice to feel dead-sure that wasn't written by you."

Pinn's silence accepted acquittal. "So that's Moloney?" Brumby nodded his head up and down, contracting the nostrils as if to keep out a smell.

"Mind," said Pinn, weighing the words out, in scrupulous fairness to all, "I don't say the man writes well—as far as mere form goes."

"Well, no," said Brumby, much as a creditor takes, on account, a first penny in the pound.

Pinn had to go on paying. "—nor, perhaps, that his is a genial nature."

"Good Lord!" Only another farthing!

No more came, though. Pinn's imperious conscience now informed him that only the extremities of an underling's person may be law-fully thrown to the wolves. "Still, I will say"—his tall upper lip came down like a drop-curtain—"that that man has a stern, an almost sombre rigour of conviction—" The other groaned.

Of what fiend of the nether pit could this black zealot speak so? "—reminding me often," Pinn ground on, "of the granite, the native English granite of a Cromwell." He was growing excited. The granite metaphor, got from an old speech of Bright's, was one of the three or four figures of speech that had ever gone to Pinn's head; it's use always made him a little unsteady.

Another groan. Brumby would just like to see the beast; at least, so he thought, as one thinks one would not mind a look at the Gorgon. "Well!" with a strain he stomached his just repugnance. "So long as you don't put him on very often—"

"Often? My dear sir, one does one's own work," Pinn said austerely.

"And what man wouldn't?" Brumby replied with an answering dignity. So deep calleth unto deep. That instant their souls stood together; the next, the unresting messenger came in again and laid down some sheets of paper. He had a good voice, well produced, that messenger. When he said "Mr. Fay's leader, sir," nothing was lost.

Pinn, in the ebb of his tortures, was not in case precisely to whistle; still, the breath, checked by the words of the messenger, had to escape; it made almost an "Ah!" Then Brumby, the old early riser to crises, rose. One basilisk glance at the boy was all that he yielded to weakness. It was gone and then he was one who has just brought off the pretty surprise he had, long ago, secretly rigged for a friend.

"See that!" He merrily brandished Fay's work under the nose of Moloney's employer. Now, don't ever fancy again you're the only man in the world who knows only too well that to get a thing done as you want you must do it yourself. Not"—the sportsman in him loyally added—"but Fay has his points, poor chap. If I must be off duty, some two or three nights, or whatever it is, in the month, I dare say I might do worse than let him have a shot at the thing—"

"I see," said Pinn. He was wishing he did. Could it be this Fay, this hired stabber in the dark, that Brumby's frankness was tempering any excess in previous eulogy. "I do admit he's a bit of a hitter when his blood's up; like the dervishes, you know—a bit fanatical; he's apt to feel the things he writes; that's what it is; gets carried away."

"I see," said Pinn again grimly.

And, the next moment, he did. For Brumby, with a sudden recurrence of joviality, poked at his thorax. "'Pedant'—eh? 'Sophist'—eh?

'Compost,' was it? Ha! Ha!" In the one breath the sane man of the world playfully chid Pinn's sensitiveness under fire, and disowned, so far as honour allowed, Fay's too pitiless heats of Tory conviction. "Come now," the mellower spirit seemed to say to the two crude extremes, "laugh and shake hands." But no handshaking for Pinn. Pinn shake hands with evil! Not he. "Was that his work?" he growled, with his neck hairs bristling.

Brumby nodded pleasantly, deprecating any grudges. "Mind you," he said, "a good chap in his way." A grunt came from Pinn. "But he's earnest—that's it; it's that overdone craze about 'principle.'" Pinn glared. Nice ghostly consolation, this, for an outraged person of principle. "No, I'm not crying down principle, either," Brumby ambled along, with liberal concessiveness, feeling his balm had not wholly soothed; "I always say it's a perfectly justifiable thing in its place; if in other respects man is a gentleman, principle won't lead him very far wrong. Take my word for it. Only, poor Fay, you see" Again the generous fellow checked; why do more than just touch, as little as candour allowed, on the poor man's want of breeding? After all, we are all of us victims of circumstance. "Well," he broke off, "now we both know where we stand. He came nearer; something led him again to hold out his hand. Pinn took it. They met on the heights, for a moment the two tall spirits looked level into each other's eyes, the shade of the one blent with the glow of the other. Then the bell rang on the wall. It was over; they stepped down again, into our lower fife.

Ten seconds more, and Pinn, at the telephone, poured out orders of all kinds; he spoke low and fast, with his face to the wall, the whole man gummed to his work—mind, eyes, ears; nothing but it existed, for him; at least, nothing mattered; he heard, as a thing alien and indifferent, a knock at an opposite door, and entering steps; even Brumby's loud, "Oh, it's you, Fay? Through?" seemed unmomentous, though he did hear it as he turned, his telephoning done, still thinking—had he sent all the orders necessary? Yes. Then he looked round.

"Moloney! You here!"

Brumby stared wildly. "Moloney?"

Finn's eyes hunted round the room. No, there were only the three of them there. He stared back wildly at Brumby. "Fay?"

CHAPTER VII

Ex illo fluere et retro sublapsa referri
Spes Danaum, fractae vires . . .
VERGIL, Æneid, ii.

There are things not to be put on the stage; a lady killing her infants, a king putting out his own eyes— better take them as seen; one yell, if you will, from a child "off," to keep your fancy at work, one waft of sound from where Œdipus damns and blasts in the wings as he rams in the pin; but no more; blood is fine, but it pays to go straight to the more delectable mess that is made of the souls of the principals. No disrespect to suppers of horrors; only, of two, hold out for the squarer.

So be it unsaid here how it looked, how it sounded, when Pinn and Brumby found tongue and took turns to give Fay gigantic pieces of their minds. Indeed to try were of no use; who shall paint the sun, full face, at noon? The radiant heat and light of their joint and several rages had that ardour; they beat down on the wicked; like a worm that has strayed on the gravel they dried him up almost to nothing, him and his humours. Besides, one would scarcely dare. You do not report High Mass; here was a commination service, the Dies Irae, only on earth; common wrongs made the two celebrants one, as with a sacrament; Pinn, the Baptist, detonated with Athanasian fury; Brumby, one of the Church's foundations, talked conscience like a Nonconformist. Did the like of you or me pull out a sketch-book to draw on the spot these angels of wrath spreading their wings on the blast, we might justly feel we were all but brawling in church. Enough that vengeance was theirs; out went the unclean thing from the camp, the two camps drummed into outer darkness.

Not a word, while the rite lasted, had the two just men said to each other. And yet, how intimately had they communed. Every bang at the drum, each knew, was a pledge; every censure a vow, and each brace made the vow mutual; both were sworn, without a word said, to fast not from Fay only, but from all such abhorred meats. Enough, for them, of the potential Fays of this world. Each had the other's word that vicarious generalship was over; no more of these proxy bell-wethers, whatever the weight of the bell; let the common, unwriting editor, elsewhere, do as he would, these two would go back to the jannock Halland tradition; no guiding word that came as from either of them would come, on the way, through another brain but his; once again they would literally give their best; they would give themselves.

Pinn, to say nothing of Brumby, found it in him to be almost glad of the cleansing fire, that night, as he curled up in bed—for so far he was human; he curled. For one last time they had had to make use of the poison; it had been too late, that night, to replace Fay's trash; both papers were all but out when the rogue was caught. All the effort lay in front, and both fell asleep as happy in their strength for it as men who feel, with a skinful, the iron will with which they will spurn strong liquor the rest of their lives. It was no mere hugging of fancies, either. Next day Brumby, for one, strode down to his office, as the strong man rejoiceth to run a race, framing, as he strode, the few brusque, straight-flung words with which for the next few days he should head off any intrusive compliments on the new fire of the Warder's leaders. Arrived, he proceeded to light it. Hard work it was, too; strange, when it came to writing, how many points had to be looked up and got, in a paltry sense, right—points that in talk will be turned or shunned by anyone not a bore—dates that the wise do without; intractable titles of Acts and Commissions, whole tracts of arid fact not fit to be shown in the landscape by more than a few picked dots and ends of lines charged and flashing with significance; or better, perhaps, in colour, washed in with light allusive touches of the full brush sped by the right instinct. Could some tyrant, harder than he that set Michelangelo modelling in snow, set certain impressionist painters to state, with the rigid explicitness forced on the worker in marble, the thrills that they felt before Nature, the poor men might have Brumby's sense of revolt against the world's waste or misuse of the rarest gifts of its children. Nothing higher, he soon perceived, than an insect would spin an entire cocoon like this out of its own vitals. And then his talent for organization came to his aid. Half, more than half, the staff were soon taken from the common round of their night's work; at a word from him they threw down their trivial tasks; they left all, to devil in the greater cause. Sub-editors rummaged, under direction, the offspring of the teeming minds of Whitaker, Hazell, and Dod; the chief reporter, stirring, at Brumby's circumstantial request, his stumps, ran for a Blue Book.

For the early hours of that evening Brumby sat like a Pharaoh at the building of a pyramid, thrilled by the vastness of his exertions, and keeping the coolies hard at it. Then he wrote. As the night wore on he took off first his coat, then his boots; the perspiration surprised him; but the massed materials cried out to be touched with the enchantment of perfect form; if he had to strip to the buff he would stick to it. Stick he did; he wrote, and undid buttons, till the agonized foreman compositor, a man early grey with just catching newspaper trains, came down and snatched the last page from under the current pen. Perhaps that day's Warder, the first of the new birth, had, like all of us, its failings. The diversion of so many streams of labour overnight left certain cultivable areas, no doubt, perceptively parched. Where the brief, jocund paragraph might have raised its juicy shoots, the penny-a-lining local reporter stretched his dry waste of sand. Still, as often as Brumby read the leader—and he found that after half an hour of other work he could always come back to it fresh—he felt the game was worth while.

Besides, as he got more into the thing, he would soon be able to spare more and more men for the other work of the office; their minds, no doubt, all the better for having the short release from humdrum. More; not only the thing would come easier; he meant it to come different; he meant to redeem all our modern political writing from all its delving at data and reference, chapter and verse; the thing was too fusty. What a fellow must want on the way to town these raw mornings was contact with a ripe, sun-warmed temperament; you ought to get right up against him; he should feel the glow of your nature, its lustre, fruitiness and body, its form and pressure. Brumby would see to it. No headlong changes of course; better to work towards the right thing slowly, Nature's way; and, first, simply to stop the rot, to caulk the holes the rat had been gnawing, to reassure his world that the Warder was still himself, his whole self, and nothing but himself.

For two nights had his pen testified to this, when there came by post a note on very good paper, not signed; just the words: "Gregory, remember thy swashing blow!" It was queer—not that unsigned letters should come; night and morning, foundling counsels are left on the door-step of editors; what was queer was the way this one mattered; it had a magnetic impersonality. Brumby, urged by he knew not what, sent for a Shakespeare, with notes; Tudor idiom was puzzling enough, but Tudor idiom cut out of its matrix and set in some new context that was not even given—this was Delphi quoting the Sphinx, a conundrum two deep. He craved to pooh-pooh it, and yet, yet, he went asleep that night teasing himself with the thought that he knew the writing. Asleep, he dreamt he was crossing a wide steppe, alone, and had felt on his face a first flake of snow like the man in Bret Harte, and he woke in a fright. Only a dream, of course; and next night and the next and all the following week he toiled at the salvage, letting all else slide; he did not go once to the Wigwam, his club; for ten days he had not touched a golf-club; for dinner he failed two hostesses.

Saturday, Sabbath of Jew and journalist, came again. Even then, on his trade's rest-day, letters came up to his house, sent on from the office; at breakfast the first thing he saw on his plate, as a sick man sees blood again in his phlegm, was his name in the haunting handwriting. There had been an election in Halland the day before; all the week he had conjured the faithful to quit them like men; his pen, a very sword, had been everywhere; it had flashed at the head of the van; it had whipped in the flanks; those who skulked in the rear he beat with the flat. All had been done that man could do; only, the Midianites were very many; all was done in vain. He opened the letter. In it there were, at the top, the calamitous figures of yesterday's rout, and below them, as if the man could not leave his quoting alone:

O for one hour of Wallace wight,
Or well-skilled Bruce to rule the fight
And cry "Saint Andrew for our right!"
Another sight had seen that morn,
From Fate's dark book a leaf been torn,
And Flodden had been Bannockbourne!

Suddenly he knew the writing; recognition slipped into his mind as your heel when all but past hope of insertion, slips into a boot. The hand, he could swear, was that of the Sheriff, his eulogist six days ago; he that had praised the ghost blamed the living man. Poor old Sheriff; even the great ones of the earth must mind where they put their feet, else they may come these croppers. Well, he would not tell tales on the Sheriff; anonymity was a trap to lay; what it caught should have mercy. While his thoughts earned him the fifth beatitude, his hands opened another letter and another, and then a third. This arrested him:

DEAR MR. BRUMBY,

For God's sake cure your cold, or mumps, or colly-wobbles—I don't mind the least what it is—and come back to work and sack the wishy-washy windbag of an understudy that's been on the job this week. All we want is just a little plain English common sense from some one who means what he says and says what he means. In fact we want you. Excuse plainness, and believe us.—Your faithful,

COUNTRY MANNERS.

So, then, it was snow; the flakes thickened. But O blind generation! that loved him and yet did not know him for certain, called on his name in their hours of doubt and trouble, and took for the true deliverer the first ventriloquist that answered to it. Moses could not be off duty an hour; the people would set to and say their prayers to a calf. Out, too, on Fay more than ever, Fay that had aped him to his hurt, taking from the true mint its recipe for coining in gold and forging with it shams that cut the gold out in the hearts of its lovers, debauching their sight with a yellow more garishly telling, till the sheen of the real thing fell dull on their eyes. No, no, though; let us be fair; on the eyes of some, a few, strays, incompetents. After all, the rest had their faculties left. To-night, he remembered with pleasure, he dined with Hedlum, the head of the Bar in Halland, not a Conservative, certainly—no Liberal either—and yet the man for his mood, an impregnable rock of normal practical wisdom, one of the power-stations of our English life, ever generating the sober sagacity that makes world's go round. Basking in the radiance of Hedlum's sanity, his own trust in the innate decency of men, in the mass, would pick up the tone it had lost at the touch of the poor freaks, high and low, who had just been airing their insensibility.

Hedlum was not a freak, certainly. "Thou art a blessed fellow," the Prince said to Poins, "to think as every man thinks; never a man's thought in the world keeps the roadway better than mine." More blessed still, Hedlum took twenty per cent off what every man thought, and the rest he affirmed, with a contained momentum; then every man felt how right, in the main, he had been, and Hedlum even more right than he—so regally, affluently right that the luxury of under-statement was well within his means. Hedlum would take up all that was current, trim it and pare its nails and give it his blessing and send it out into the world to get on, and it did, famously; the day's buzz of common thought and talk paid tithes of its total volume for leave to rebound from a mind so sonorous; and not a bad bargain either. When the residue came echoing back from that judicial-looking bench you felt that if it was not true, then the fault was truth's; at least, there must be some upper order of truth, not universally known, to which he had conformed and to which the facts, in the vulgar sense, could not have been loyal.

All of him helped the effect. He was of the settled age, fifty or so, handsome with the controlled benignity, the mellowed precision, the happy, distinguished, melancholy sometimes united in a good-looking judge. His blue spectacles gave you thoughts of Homer, Milton, the whole venerable company of sightless seers in books, as you watched the weighing of each word at its exit from the shaved, working lips, or the closure of their inexorable adamant behind its heels. As the last commonplace of club gossip, smoke-room heroics, or music-hall sentiment issued from these portals, transfigured by the moderate discount that made it twice itself, you not only saw it was final truth, or virility's quintessential emotion; you felt he had done something decisive, even gallant, and that you were in it, a fine fellow, too, in your way; and you quickened; you lived back and forward, back to the blithe days at school when they first taught you never to think your own thoughts or take what came in a way of your own, but to pool your brains with the rest and "throw yourself into the life of the school," and on to your early manhood's deeper training in resemblance to others, and so to the good day, always coming and always here, always to be had by him who wills it with his might, when the imitative shall inherit the earth.

Brumby's fishing for counsel's opinion at dinner that night was not good. It showed no finesse; he had not the coolness. With joyless humour he led on through talk of the odd things editors see, the faddists they have to keep down, the cranks to head off, to the droll little hits that are made at them out of the dark by wild men; why, only this week he had twice been taunted with not being quite the man that he had been five days ago. Curse old Hedlum! Why need he stop laughing like that? Why should he say,

"Well, well!" in that balancing tone, with that enigmatic tolerance—it might be for the assassins, it might be for some poor wretch that had failed from out his blood, in his hour of trial.

"Yes?" Brumby asked almost pettishly.

Hedlum was majestically slow. He finished his claret and leant back, feeling about for a gentleman's way to be cruel, only to be kind—the phrase filled his whole mind, as the key-phrase of a situation always did. "Don't you think, sometimes," he started at last, with his sweetly reasonable stop full on, "that perhaps we all may, for a season, be something short of our fullest selves? Hedlum's humility had a cogent grandeur; think of Solon, for argument's sake, owning himself the makings of a klepto-maniac. You could not go on arguing. "I am bound to say," Hedlum went on, "frankly, that if anyone were to ask me, on my oath, if I found in the Warder to-day—in the Stalwart either, for that matter"—Hedlum loved these parenthetic advertisements of immunity from bias—"quite the same fairly high and clear note of authority that each has led us to expect—from the Warder, that of a strong and attractive personality; from the Stalwart, that of rigorously cohesive thought—well, I confess—Then Brumby knew that the clubs, the Bar messes, the whole noble army of diners-out—how dear they all were to him!—were lost. Not that he put it to himself, articulately that Hedlum echoed them. But Brumby knew. Hedlum's sovereign sanity was theirs, squared, cubed. But with the killing thought came another, not killing. Pinn was losing hold too.

"For instance?" he asked, the raw place craving alike for the torturing hand and for this new oil that might drip from it.

"That's a very fair question," said Hedlum suavely; if you have been in the courts you will know the tone of surprised judicial commendation of a prisoner's rational conduct of his own defence. He looked through a little heap of old newspapers. "This will do," he said, and took one; "I'll spare your blushes; I'll draw my proof from the Stalwart of ten days ago—from its leader on that speech of Albry's; but mind, every word I say in its praise applies, mutatis mutandis, to things of your own, at your best." He folded the paper to read. "I'll skip the exordium," he said; "it just states the case. Then the writer goes on."

And so, with intention and gusto, the vir pietate gravis, the image of reason and conscience at friends with the world, read out the second, or middle, part of a leader that you know of, adorning with forensic fullness and roundness of stress every worn tag of verbiage that reeked, beyond the common, of the bluster, timorousness, false finality of meanly gregarious half-minds.

"'We are forced to stale the point at issue in this some-what plain and bald fashion because there has grown up so noticeable an aversion to the cold touch of realities in the minds of those who know only too well how soon a plain tale would set them down.

"In words, like weeds, they wrap them o'er,
Like coarsest cloak against the cold.

That cloak we are forced to tear away. The time for words is past. At last we are face to face with a definite, practical issue. ' "

"You see," Hedlum put in, taking off his spectacles a moment and looking blandly at the listener, before going on, "how he hits the nail on the head; how he confronts us with the actual.

"'The lists are set; the trumpet has sounded; which is it to be?'"

"It stirs one like a trumpet, really," the reader interpolated again, and went on:

"'Is the verdict which has already been passed in the minds of all right-thinking men to be formally entered and acted upon as the verdict of the whole community? Or are we to witness one more instance of the occasional inability of fairly intelligent communities to express at once, in their public acts, the ripest thoughts and sanest feelings of their nobler part?'"

"The writer never loses his balance, you see—is never carried away. He masters himself." I go on:

"'In these days of feverish haste and multiple pre-occupation it is hard to tell what may not happen'—"

Nothing short of exhaustive italicization would express Hedlum's relish for this piece of profundity. He pursued:

"'—yet we cannot resist the conclusion that even if a blow be not struck now for a considered and coherent conception of the public interest, the inevitable growth of a sober public opinion will intervene at last to mitigate if it may not avert, the consequences of a passing lapse from civic duty in its truest and highest sense.'"

He looked up, placid, assured, majestic, in generous reliance on Brumby's recognition of great qualities, even in an enemy. "It goes on," he said, reading more lightly, as if in mere annotation of a proved case:

"'Enough has been said to leave no doubt as to the nature and the importance of the issue at stake, and we are loth to add even one word that might seem to travel beyond the cardinal question of facts, and in the direction of personalities.'"

"However, perhaps I needn't read more, to answer your question. O si sic omnia!—that's all I say." He paused a moment, hesitating between the pangs of suppressed quotation and the lofty instinct of abstention from further improvement of a secured triumph. The pangs had it, and he quoted gravely and melodiously:

"'Though deep, yet clear; though gentle, yet not dull;
Strong, without rage; without o'erflowing, full.'

"Above all—straight." The word, in Hedlum's fine voice, was like the last note of an organ; the silence after hung down from it, letting go finger by finger reluctantly. Hedlum enjoyed the cadence down to its last vibration. Then, with a true sense of contrast, he put on the bright, breezy, brotherly stop. No young curate with the hue of his agreeable, athletic boyhood as yet unsicklied by thought or study could be more didactically cheery.

"And you're just as straight, just as strong, my dear Brumby, in your own way, when your pen is itself. Come now, give it its rights. Let yourself go, again. Give us the old bracing tone, the grit, the moral originality, the keen, tonic air, as of Alpine heights. Take it from me—and I think you safely may—that no one in England better knows how."

Whenever Hedlum said: "Take it from me," he was happy. It meant, like a certain Greek particle, that he who used it was a mighty and spreading oak under whose umbrageous wisdom the person addressed was free to huddle from the rain in which, by his own error, he was then out. "Foolish virgin," it explained, "here is oil; take some, gratis. I have plenty." But thoughts, rodent past cure by such ministrations, were getting their teeth into Brumby. What if Pinn at that moment were hearing things like these? Pinn, with all allowances made, was but a sorry, desiccated soul, void of honest bowels of good fellowship; not one instinct of a sportsman in him to keep him from running outside the posts, if he were unwatched. The dog returns to its vomit. Was Pinn sneaking back in the dark at that moment, his tail licking under his belly, to re-swallow Fay?

CHAPTER VIII

Doth any man doubt, that if there were taken out of men's minds vain opinions, flattering hopes, false valuations, imaginations, as one would, and the like, but it would leave the minds of a number of men poor shrunken things, full of melancholy and indisposition, and un-pleasing to themselves?
BACON, Essay of Truth

No, Pinn had not come to that; to him no one had written; no bludgeoning friend had left him covered, like Brumby, with faithful weals. But by now Pinn could have almost wished that, say, one friend had tried—not a gang, but just one—to make a break in a sense that he had of making a speech in a full morgue, where no one could rise to the points—that, or else a vast, vacuous cave where his voice went bounding, rebounding about from wall to wall, investigating the solitude.

Each night he wrote what he felt to be powerfully winged words; each morning, so far as the eye could see, they flew forth with the right centrifugal vigour in the Stalwart's familiar red carts; and yet, though all might be well, his own eyes could not see the glory of its being well, as they had done when the mechanic, routine parts of the prophetic office, the mere voice production, the verbal arrangement of his message to the age were otherwise provided for, and the prophet himself was left to move freely among both the children of light and those of this world, and to note the diverse incidence of final truth on the mind open to good and on hard shells. How could his soul now enjoy good in his labour? It had not the time. Hard work is a regular veld, for loneliness; as Pinn stalked on across it, panic began to hang over him, a vulture not yet at his eyes, only hovering high in the air, under the sun, in great curves that drew themselves on the ground in rings of circling shadow.

You are not to think that all of Fay's leaders, like that one, were made for all time and all themes and the use of any party to any of earth's quarrels. That one, indeed, although not the first of its neutral gender, had taken him time. Pains, greater than you or I might suppose, were needed, to scour out every word that might be to the point—to some point or other. But, under these labours, two things sustained him:

one, the pure, aesthetic delight to his soul of the new figures cut by Pinns and Brumbys under this perfected moonlight of Puckishness; the other, the earthlier prudence of husbands and fathers. For ours, the economists said, was an epoch of "interchangeable parts"; in the younger days of farm machinery a reaper that got out of order in Connaught might have to go home to where it was born—to Bedford or Norwich, perhaps—to be mended; now, the farmer had nothing to do but write for some "standardized" piece that would fit into any reaper; with that he could put the thing right in ten minutes. Had not the march of mind brought us on to the point when nuts, bolts and cogged wheels in the mechanism of government by talk should be standardized also, and the toiling harvester in that field, too, delivered from half of his unforeseen fixes? Hence Fay's experiments; not that he thought of cleaving solely to the new model; rather his mind ran on two concurrent departments, like those of the tailors—"bespoke" and ready-made.

For emergency nights, and for nights when composition was distasteful, Fay thought he would keep by him always a stock of stout slop suits to fit all the normal and constant controversial states of mind; any great cause that came fuming and raging at any time into the shop could then be sent happy away in a reach-me-down rig, at the end of five minutes. And yet the putting of glove-fits on Brumby and Pinn was too near the craftsman's heart to be quite given up. For each angle of Pinn's scraggy spirit, for each more curvilinear protuberance of the beefy soul of Brumby, it had long piqued Fay to fashion a portraying expression of itself, at first with the irony of literal precision, and then with the heightening, stressing glee of the painter who itches to make his sitters more like themselves than they are, to teach Nature to articulate, and each salient trait of temper and basic trick of thought to work itself out on the face without the hesitant blur of "real" life. To make these halves the wholes they might be, to give to dull spite the fullest use of its wits, to cocksureness all of its estate of brass, to the pedant and the virilist their several rights of stark rigidity and of jolly brutishness—to these works of love (for he did, in a way, love not only the work but the things he worked on, as Swift loved his fops, and Darwin the worms) Fay was inflamed by the natural value of the contrast between his models; it was fun to polish that up and stud it with extra points, like a story good to begin with. All of Brumby that played the dog to the cat of Pinn Fay patiently rendered more canine, and Pinn more feline, to match; Brumby he purged, as he went on, of anything like coherent thinking; from Pinn she queezed out any last oozings of blood or humour. In a couple of years he had put the two positive types through both degrees of comparison; each now shone before men with a light that, from being more Brumbian, or more Pinnish, than it was, had waxed ultra-Brumbian, super-Pinnish, more Brumbian or Pinnish than it could ever have been with no Fay to raise it to the nth. power of itself.

All who witnessed the transfiguration were stirred; none, however, more deeply than Pinn. Reading his own Stalwart of a morning he was like them that dream; worlds of old, obstructive things got out of his way; mystic fists lunged out from him, thrice the length of his arm; he punched, with a reach not given to him in old days the remote and guarded noses of malignity and error; he was winged, as those dreamers are, and flew off down trunk roads of argument, so often tramped wearily by him in their middle stretches, to thrilling termini of finality. A thin lucidity, austere reason, syllogistic morals, all his bony harem of veiled mistresses undid the baffling lawn and fired him with the view of countenances parched and unsensuous to his heart's desire.

To put forth all one's strength may be merely to take from oneself half the good of it. Cook your own dinner, know just what is coming up, and, whatever your gift in the art, rapture is gone; the delicious enigma of the dish-covers is as a tale that is told. Had you but planted the sacred fire of your leading ideas in the heart of a competent cook, and left the thing there!

It now dawned on Pinn that verbal inspiration may be too plenary for the peace of the divine mind that lays it on. His organ, so far as it had lived for that good end, was ceasing to be organic. Intrinsically, of course, the force of a dominant brain must be used to more purpose directly than through an attorney. But what good, pray, had he of it? A novel impulse was on him, to rush out among people, anywhere, away from this awesome cohabitation with his own powers in a resonant vacuum. He held out a while, but Monday morning, the one after Brumby's dinner with Hedlum, found the impulse ungovernable.

To the friends of the popular cause he had served out, the night before, the usual jorums of argumentative rum; to-day his Stalwart was not unfolded; his own lips abhorred the stuff. He sent for Bradshaw, picked a train, and flung out of doors, making for Over Belton, down the estuary. Belton was sore Halland's bath, her Margate. He knew the name; there would be crowds there.

In the train, at first, there was balm. Of four men in the compartment, all of them strangers, and three of them clearly golfers bound for the Belton links, two had the Stalwart; one of them read it, the other slept, with each end of a copy tucked rug-wise under each femur; only one had a Warder; the fourth nourished reason on the Dead Snip, or One-Horse Mammoth, an organ of prophecy, chief bread-winner of the Halland bookmakers. Stalwart and Warder, joined in these just proportions, brought back the thrill of that night, the steely glitter of his own scorn, the credit that Brumby had done himself too— poor, muddy cursing, no doubt, but then, think of the man; waters, by a law of Nature, cannot rise higher than their source; and then the deject tail of the goat shooed in the wilderness; and, last of all, and less balmy, the infinitesimal fear lest that tail, as it went, was tipped for one second with just the least curl of a contumacious waggle.

"Done with the Stalwart?" the Warder man asked of his opposite, who had now ceased to read.

"Bear to see the Warder?" he added offering the exchange.

Both read again. Their friend, having honourably carried self-control well over the frontiers of sleep, now lost hold, and snored frankly, till a "Good Lord, deliver us!" broke in tones of vivacious disgust from the student of the Stalwart.

"Litany too, by George!" groaned the sleeper, awaking. He stared, blinking, gradually relieved. "If I didn't dream I was in church! And the Stalwart turned parson and preaching—a fat pi haw about moderation! Fact is, a man can't be too careful about what he reads before going to bed." As sleep and its terrors drew back, he grew lively. "What has gone wrong with the Stalwart, that's what I want to know. Hewlitt now, you ought to know; you're a Radical."

"With the Stalwart?" As he stressed the name, the man addressed gave a basilisk look at the Warder he had in his hands.

"Yes, your dear Stalwart," cut in the original petitioner to Heaven. "Why, the thing's half dead: hasn't the life to be nasty; not a snort left in it."

"That's right," concurred the ingrate who had slept with the Stalwart warming his reactionary thighs; "Hewlitt, my boy, it's a serious affair. Here are we Tories paying our penny a day to see the heathen rage, and I'm hanged if he's raging. I tell you, we're not getting value."

"Are we, d'you think, we Liberals?" Hewlitt retorted with a glance that, again, might have burnt a hole in the Warder he held.

But the litanist's preoccupation with his own wrongs swept him past interruption. "Question is," he said, "granted the Stalwart has got to talk rot of some sort, it being a party rag, can't it at any rate talk rot like a man—crisp, nervous, Anglo-Saxon rot, the way it used to, not wishy-washiness like this?" He took the paper from his knees and read, with ribald stress on each balancing and qualifying word:

"'If it cannot be honestly said that the Premier completely justified all the opinions he advanced last night, it must at least be allowed that there is more force than he himself possibly realizes in his contention that a good many factors in the present situation have to be taken into account in estimating the probabilities of the case.'"

And so it is for this that a man may trace, with a stern, self-curbing vigilance, every nick in the indented coast of truth. The scoffer, no doubt, was only a malignant and an obscurantist—a buffoon at that; and yet the scoff made the poor naked new-born child of Pinn's invention seem other than it was, so much does the quality of made things live in the percipient eye and perish at its perversion. Scientific exactitude, imperturbable balance, irresistible moderation—a passing clown breathed in their face and they shrivelled to a skeleton system of blanks, a void syllabus of nullities.

The other clown was at it now, riding his crass jest to a standstill, clown-fashion. "There!" he exulted. "Call that a pennyworth? Call that heathen rage of the kind and quality demanded by the purchaser? I suppose it's what Rads would call 'sane.' It's what I call a breach of the Food and Drugs Act. Sane I We'll be having Hewlitt sane next!"

A fond paternal roar from the author of this sally, echoed by the thinker who had read aloud, duly identified brisk incivility with wit. But Hewlitt, a wiry, hard-bitten veteran of club chaff was not done with. "You won't," he rejoined, "if you play off a Warder upon me each time I take you down to the links. Why, the thing just tears round and round in a circle. It makes your head turn. Listen. Mind, I don't cry up the Stalwart. It's gone all to bits, I grant, since that fire; Pinn's top floor was gutted, perhaps. Still Pinn does say something. But the Warder—nothing I Absolutely nothing I Listen:

"'It is easy to exaggerate the significance of such a speech as the Prime Minister's, as indeed it is to under-rate its importance.'"

"You see—plus and minus—cancel out—nothing left!

"'Whether reform cannot come more advantageously by tackling practically some of the difficulties that confront us is a question that we must leave to be determined by the general sense of those whose political opinions rest on a serious study of affairs.'"

"Now, what does that say? Anything? Or nothing? I ask anyone."

The triumphant query in his face challenged them all. For the moment the two friends of the constitution were stuck; the amateur of prophecy detached his eyes from the Dead Snip, and offered a look of imbecile receptiveness; Pinn before he knew, had said "Not much, certainly, with a wintry smile. So that was how Brumby wrote. Strangely, he had not looked at the Warder all the past week. He would buy one at Belton. The train was slowing for it. The session broke up.

If you would view fair Melrose aright, go visit it by the pale moonlight; if Belton, visit it at Whitsuntide, when on the level shore young Halland brooks the hardy ass, when the brave and the fair chaff and squeal, change hats, acquire coconuts with their good right hands, or, squatted on the sand dunes, sit out midsummer suns in silent ecstasies or agonies of mutual appreciation or embarrassment. August over, Belton goes down, like Persephone, into a chilled hell of her own; the sands, that were so full of people, sit desolate; serried ranks of penny-in-the-slot machines, enough to keep all Halland herself in goodies and knowledge of her weight, stand rusting; like the arches derelict in the Campagna they speak mournfully of man's presence and of his passing. As winter advances, on the high, narrow ledge of concrete piled, between the tea-rooms and the beach, by the giant hands of the District Council, the Belton landladies, urged by famine,* range in and out and back and forth, seeking whom they may provide, by a kind of violence, with a plain tea, or calling aloud on reason and justice to applaud their several tariffs for the extras that have justly won for the ledge the name of Eggs-and-Bacon esplanade. Pinn had never seen Belton before, True, he lived only ten miles away. But some of his holidays had to be spent at Grindelwald, threatening reluctant Christendom with a reunion of all churches; others at Biarritz, making it clear by his aspect that he was not there as an idler or seeker of pleasure; others in Florence, Venice, Umbria, firmly enduring the arts and deepening his sense of the enormity of the Roman error. So the democrat never had thrust himself upon Demos in his seaside pleasaunce. But he knew, through print, as he knew most things which he knew at all, that Belton, generally speaking, was thronged with the "masses." Print always said so, as ancient print always has said the Buccleugh was bold; a depopulated watering-place or a nervous Buccleugh being, as the gifted minds at the back of the printed word perceived, too charmless for commemoration.

—"quas improba ventris
Exegit caecas rabies, catulique relicti
Faucibus expectant siccis.'
VERGIL, Ænid.

Print being right, by the law of its nature, Pinn saw, more clearly than ever, that life had gone wrong— not of course, to spite him, but still in a way that would try any man—when he emerged from the station into a very fair copy of Tadmor in the wilderness. The shops, though unshuttered, were deathly still; in the one where he bought a Warder, the proprietor, when roused, moved as in a secular trance; in the boulevardian street some one in knickers was, with the indomitable spirit of youth, walking out a fox-terrier; in the vacant roadway a man in the late evening of life stood stock still, simply drawing his breath, adoring the wintry sunshine, and enduring numbly till, like the column relieving Lucknow, one o'clock dinner should burst into sight. Horror ubique animos, simul ipsa silentia tenent.

Hailed from all sides by the echoes of his boots, Pinn traversed the ringing piazza at the pier-end; thence to gain the beach he had only to run the blockade of the maenads on their ledge. His looks were his safety; any man less stupefyingly glum might well have been torn to as many pieces as Orpheus, and each piece accommodated with the best eighteen penny lunch in Belton; Pinn passed alive and unfed; the last poignant cries of unsatisfied hospitality died down behind him; beyond, on the open shore, a solitary nursemaid trailed, melancholy as a thaw, over desert spaces of sand, listlessly desiring her charges, as she turned each new page of her novelette, to come out of that puddle and not catch their deaths; beyond her was solitude.

He had come out to look for a multitude, to rub against it, to feel it was there. Then, for a time, after the first disappointment, he hardly craved for his kind at all. Man, as seen, in sample, in the train, was not to be coveted in bulk. It was one thing for Crusoe to feel the need of society; another to see the first print of a beastly savage's foot on the sand. It was enough to walk on alone and think of Brumby. For Brumby, it seemed, was not coming off with the mob any better than he. Well, with the mob what it was, Brumby's state was so much the more gracious, though none could deny that the specimen read in the train was poor beyond palliation, whoever the judge. Best, anyhow, that Brumby should now go on in that vein; whatever its other shortcomings, at least it would not disturb the balance of power in the Halland press; Providence, had it been less infinitely good, might have made Brumby a prodigy of bad readableness, trashily facetious, spicily pert, a Roman candle of flash paradoxes, alluring to the untutored mind; the clear-eyed Power that might have taught cows to bite and given horses long, sharp horns had so framed Brumby that while he fumbled at his tools a serious thinker might have time, without any exposure to sordid anxieties, to make it plain, and even interesting, to a befogged generation that its every act should be the conscious application of some reasoned moral principle.

By the time the hard walking and eager thinking had raised his spirits a little, Pinn had reached Bardolph's Conk, the jutting point of red sandstone that ends the home reach of Belton sands. Beyond it there opens out—unseen till you pass the Conk—the mile-long Laggo Bay, a crescent of white sand changed that day into something rich and strange by the sea's infinite jest and excellent fancy. A Spanish steamer, feeling her way up the silted estuary in a rising wind, the evening before, had grounded on Laggo Bank, a mile out; the captain and crew came ashore; there was no sensation; it looked like a common case for salvage at leisure. But the wind rose to a gale in the night; as the tide fell it hammered the hull on the shoal till first her back broke and then she went right to pieces and the waves washed the cargo clean out of her hold. The wind was blowing on shore. The cargo was oranges, done up in sketchy crates; onions, in frail crates too; and wine, in the wood.

Morning broke on a curved mile of white sand fringed with a ribbon of innumerable oranges, their noble yellows melting into the mellow browns, the greens, the lucent greys, the delicate and managed blues of onions that had taken off one, or two, or more coats to the work of the night. Here and there, among these minor treasures, as judgeships shine among the lesser prizes of the Bar, a cask of sherry offered itself to English earth. Near one cask, a few lemons advertised the circumstantial benevolence of fortune.

Unto these yellow sands the people of the coast, and of much of the hinterland, came running. Imagine what would happen if on one of these mornings manna and quails were to fall in Trafalgar Square. It did happen, on the shore of Laggo Bay. Every possessor of any hollow object, every owner of any conceivable form of cubic capacity, brought it; perambulators, school-children's satchels, clothes-baskets, bonnets, coalscuttles, the human person—all were crammed in haste; an ambulance passed and re-passed, shedding fragrance; a coffin, mobilized after a hasty eviction, had done great things for a stricken family in the first grisly light of dawn. By this time the last of the wine had, as the French say, lived; but now and again you would come across traces of swift, effectual operations, traces like those you will find in a wood—the shredded snatch of fur, the disarranged grass, the slight bloodmark; here it was two or three staves of a cask, a broken bit of a hoop, a faint discoloration of the sand, a perfume delicate above oranges. One stout clinger to the skirts of happy chance, after defending a whole hogshead against the world, had frugally borne it inland on a cart.

But I speak after the flesh, as one sopping wet with its humours. Finn had them all stanched; the dry light of his intellect burnt up fancy irrelevances; on his unhampered sight, as he turned Bardolph's Conk, there broke, in its naked hideousness, simply a mile of ardent larceny, so many head of humanity playing the beast, the ape, the magpie, going straight back, at a word from their bellies, to the moral pit whence they were digged by the pains of ages; others, perhaps vilest of all, looking on amused; meaner than Gadarene swine, they laughed while the other poor wretches rushed down a steep place.

One grizzled, spectacled, middle-aged man, who looked like a sweated schoolmaster turned out to grass for a day, was fairly beaming at the squalid carnival of illegality; his very body was radiant; he squirmed, physically as pleased children squirm. To Pinn, who unconsciously halted in front of the man where he sat, and was cheerfully asked not to stand between him and the play, he broke out in puerilities; where was old Homer now, with his "unharvested sea"? Had Pinn known, till now, that there was a coast to the Hesperides' garden? Faugh!—"What about the smell?" was his maundering reply to Pinn's trenchant reminder that all this pandemonium was over a sheer loss of wealth to a world in which many lacked bread. Wasn't it worth the world's while for a whole coast to smell just once in a way, like a good dessert on a table to which there still clung memories of the most sustaining, the most salutary, of all British entrees? Nay, the imbecile drivelled on, no English dessert ever smelt like that, no departed steak and onions ever really trailed such glories behind them; what you smelt was Spain itself, sir; not oranges, but orange groves; not just the sherry decanter; Dulcinea, rather, at the wine press. Did not Pinn's charmed nose conduct his soul to mantillas and the sitters of Valasquez, to Granada, the Escurial?—"And pause, sir, one moment, to hark to the onions—how, through the revels of your sense and your imagination, the onions still sound their sane, robust note. And of what does the aggregate odour remind you? Isn't it just of Cervantes' genius, sir, the best that was ever compounded, its feet on the earth and its head in the sky, eating God's onions and drinking His wine? Well, well—"

The creature simmered; it seemed as if the articulate words were merely a petty overflow, a drop or two lipping over from some internal reservoir of roaring enjoyment. Sickened as Pinn was, he stayed a moment to help the man back to his wits by simply putting it to him that all these people were stealing. Useless. Ineptitude merely darkened to coarse immorality. "Stealing?" the lost mind said. "Yes; but Elizabethanly. Would Drake, do you think, in all his greatness, have scorned to take a galleon loaded like this? And to us it is more; it is Spain's whole treasure, the sum of all the things in which, fallen, she still is great—the orange; the large kind of onion; sherry—her imperishable trinity of summa bona. Are thy servants swine, to turn from pearls cast before them. And think, sir, what they've resisted—the temptation. This wreck is the work, the benign, the supreme, but also the unaided, work of Nature. Man's hand was not here. And yet which of us dare say that these people, so happy to-day, did not know, when that ship was coming up this estuary, that the spread you see before you was on board, and just one little light, well placed, might—you understand me?"

"I wish you good day, sir," said Pinn. Revolted at the being's fertility in morbid clowning, he strode on angrily. For a moment the schoolmaster followed with a twinkling eye the figure of the literal man, he looked so drolly as if he were fed on a diet, exclusively, of pokers; the good scholar tried to say that in Alcaics; then he took another pull at the refreshment of the greater spectacle before going home to sustain fife on the correction of some score of the undistinguished Latin prose of a grammar-school's fifth form.

Two policemen stood together, farther on, casting the eye of benevolent rule upon the labour of the gleaners. Each gleaner had his little pile, just above high-water mark, and went and came between this base and the actual firing-line of acquisition, to lay up his gains. No doubt if one of them, A, had jumped the claim of another, B, the police would have seen that he suffered no wrong. A magistrate's heart burned within Pinn; was this, he asked them in stern and low tones, the way they did their duty? They were as gentle as ushers would be to a judge who went mad in court; there was a time, they implied in soothing periphrases, to arrest, and a time to refrain from arresting. Not till he was out of hearing did the one pronounce him "the rummest perisher I ever seen," and the other underline this valuation with the one word, "Champion!" Under Pinn the earth was giving. All these, then, were they that he would have sheltered under his wings as a hen her timid, filial chickens—these rebels, these gross, randy ducklings, wallowing in moral bog-water, or quacking blatant hilarities like that grizzled immoralist yonder. Then a new panic stole upon him; no longer the mere shudder of the nerves in bodily solitude; now it was grounded horror and fright, as in the man of middle age when first he finds his communications with the camp of youth cut off behind him. "One fire drives out another's burning"; the vexations of offended reason, the shiver of the sentry when the last footfall of the guard leaves him to the night, the tremors assailing the workman long alone with his work, which may be so good or so bad—they all began to seem like pin-pricks of yesterday to one now on the point of shouting, hammering, whining to be let in at a door that had closed, he could not say how and when, between him and all good things.

He went a little inland, over the links, a public park in the rough, and sat on a bench and tried to read his Warder. It was of no use. The pangs of exclusion were jealous; they wanted all of him. A small, grave, responsible boy, with his father's dinner-basin slung in a handkerchief, and weightier burdens at his back, stopped to rest on the bench. The distracted man could no more be silent just then, even to a random child, than a sailor newly marooned could help waving his tragic shirt at the faintest semblance of a sail.

"Do you ever read the papers, my boy?" the poor longing wretch asked, with a pitiful exuberance of casualness, twitching the Warder on his knee, by way of pleading relevance, mutely.

"Ah," the lad assented, " Saturdays, when we've had supper, me and father lays on t' floor; an' mother, she reads us out t' murders in t' Star o' Eve."

"The murders? I see. Anything else?"

"Not Saturdays. Sunday mornings father did use to read t' Weekly Stalwart. He warn't agen a bit o' politics, 'e said—not in reason. There's sense in everythink, sir, ain't there?" To the young Briton political conviction was already, like the drink, a thing for the sane to dip into warily.

"There is," said Pinn gravely. Was this another cudgel beginning to sing about his ears? Each Weekly Stalwart was a reprint, with trimmings, of the six last daily portions of light and leading. Every one of those leaders he had written with his heart's blood; put it at only a pint to each, and the Weekly Stalwart would pulse with three-quarters of a gallon. " You say he used to," said Pinn, laying his head on the block. " Has he stopped?"

Down came the axe. "Ah!"—again the assentive "Ah!" of the plebs. "He done 'is bit o' that job, he 'as. Yesterday it was. 'E 'adn't 'ardly took 'is coat orf to t' paper, same 'e always did, and then' 'Ere's out of it,' 'e says, an' 'e put on 'is coat agen. 'I'm shut o' politics,' 'e says. 'I did use to believe they was a fair fight any'ow, all in to win an' both sides tryin'; but they ain't,' 'e says to mother an' me; 'ere's this bloke as writes t' Stalwart,' 'e says, ' not 'ittin'—not to call 'ittin'—no more'n a fly, an' squared at that. An' God 'elp us,' 'e says. 'It's a wicked world; you can't put a bit on a 'orse but 'e's roped, same as this 'ere bleeder writin' in t' paper. 'Erbert, my boy,' 'e says, 'there ain't no bony fidy anywhere,' 'e says, 'outside t' murders,' and I'm to bring 'im 'ome a P'lice News Saturdays, 'stead of t' Weekly Stalwart.''

Pinn took it all as a fully thrashed horse will take a final subsidiary blow thrown in as a bonus. How all occasions, he numbly felt, did conspire against him! Even out of the mouths of babes and sucklings, or the next thing to them, was ordained consputation. The boy plodded off under his fardels, leaving in his wake the ravages of a Tamburlaine; first, that numbness of the creature cudgelled weary; then, again, a vivacity of torture that made the numbness seem as kind as a past anodyne. He was cut off; that was the horrible thing; he seemed to be entering into a sort of death: "For them that are joined to the living there is hope"—joined to the soiled, naughty, living, sustaining world by even so mean an umbilical cord as Fay. Through Fay his, touch on others had been, at any rate, that of a live man; while it was that it might still be made the touch of himself. But now—! The marooned soul was breaking down into hysterics; it ran up and down the shores of its empty islet, shrieking and praying to the speck diminishing on the horizon.

CHAPTER IX

Hostess.—O Jesu, he doth it as like one of these harlotry players as ever I see.
SHAKESPEARE, King Henry IV

These commotions, of course, were within. All that Brumby could see, at first, as he crossed the links, from the golf club's pavilion, was somebody sitting, bent down, on a bench; he seemed to be doggedly reading a newspaper. Which one? Brumby wondered dully. He too, if not in the deep waters of despair, waded its marshes. His first round of golf, since the smash, was just over and badly played too; care, that killed every life of the cat's, makes short work of that volatile tint, the pink of condition; staleness was on him, so that to-night he must hit, unfit, the mark he had missed in the prime of good training. Then, with a start, he saw it was Pinn.

The two had not met since that night of heroic generosities. Next day the Stalwart had made shift to fend for herself; some sort of jury rig was run up—enough to give Pinn a bridge to walk of his own; there is no lasting comfort in ruling the waves from the enemy's quarter-deck; better a bum-boat in fee simple.

Pinn looked up, but not with a start. Brumby—There—? Of course he was there; to have him there, flesh and all, was not strange; only mystic-ally natural; it followed; so much of him, all that counted, had been there this hour past, and the rest near; importunate desire had compelled it up so close to the outer verge of bodily sense that to see him whole was only to let go a held breath and feel again, "The world is one; yes, all of it fits."

"Too kind of you!" Brumby pointed to Pinn's Warder, the standing gruffness of his manliness a little thickened by present opaqueness of spirit.

Pinn, in all the time he had sat there, had read, in fact, nothing. But now a great thing befell him as he lay stretched out, relaxed and receptive, on the bed-like goodness of that first miracle, Brumby's coming, a miracle soft and warm, right and normal and as it should be, like all good miracles, which are never surprises—only completions. To get at Brumby, to brace him up, to be sure at least that Brumby was not back, wallowing in the mire, nay, buying up all the mire to wallow in—tired out with that longing, Pinn threw himself down to rest one moment on its fulfilment. Of course it had come; all things have rest; no tired day but has its evening. And then as he lay there, open, another miracle, trailed by the first, slipped in at some unbarred door of the mind—a lifted, gay sense of something not himself that was roughing out his purposes, for him to shape to a finish, showing him too, how to shape them, holding his hands in place, prompting him, taking him, while he went to work, right out of an old, clogged world where "Ought I?" waited, nagging, upon "I would"; what he wished became in him as a child, it was freed, it made for its end, across country; his spirits rose for the jumps. "The nobleness of life is to do this," said Antony, and kissed Cleopatra. With almost a pride in his blood, Pinn heard some tall spirit, escaped from the clay that had been his answering Brumby with effortless point. The words thrilled him; what life and edge the voice had!

"Caught out, fairly! No denying it! Leader page, too, I'm afraid. Confound you, stealing up on a man like that." It was said with a will, not quite his. Speech sat in a rudderless boat, or drifted down uncharted streams of strange fluency, alien idiom; it came on bluffnesses, abruptnesses, ellipses foreign to him; and he let, it; resistance, long tired, was drugged; it slept on guard in a mind itself awake, aflame, like capitulating sex, with a voluptuous self-surrender. "We are the clay and thou art the potter," he mentally murmured, in luxury; and aloud, to Brumby, he said, "I was just buried in it."

"Well, well," said Brumby, with the higher sincerity that disdains the weakness of a hum-bugging parade of modesty; "if it comes to that, why not?"

"Why not?" The gift at riot in Pinn snatched up the words like a cue, a licence to flow, a surface to play over. It ran on, it embroidered, it frolicked out into fantasies. "Why not? That's what I keep thinking. Why not, so long as, deep down"—and half of him stood off, charmed, and saw its twin half lightly put hand to the site of the heart in the body—"so long as, deep down, I am true to my own creed. And so I am, mind; so I am." He drew himself up, an Ajax defying the lightnings of a Zeus, even in owning his presence. "Write away; do your worst; pen of men and angels too, if you like. I don't care. I'll die the Reformer I've been all my life. Not that I say I don't read all you write, all these days. I'll not say I'm invulnerable. Only, don't think you're converting me. You're not."

He paused; not that he was gravelled; only, the fiery soul was working out its way somewhat fast for its clay tenement; he took a breather and a survey, one of the wide, slow surveys you take in an infinitesimal time when the mind is at the right heat, as long dreams are dreamt through in a second, and stored years of consciousness counted and re-packed at ease in the moment's climax of a hard race, and whole lives, they say, re-lived in one instant of the stir of a meeting with death. So perhaps, the mind of a hare coursed the first time, may have its mood of musing leisure, and stand apart, as if disinterested, watching the agony, and wondering where did its old acquaintance, the body, learn all these wonderful doublings.

But Pinn had his breath again now. "You see, it's a fad of mine. Time I was at school, fencing in the gym., I'd get so taken with the other fellow's wrist-work that I'd drop my own foil, pretty nearly, to look at him—sheer joy to see a thing done well." How did he come to say that? How did he know how to? The onlooking side of him wondered. His hand had no more touched foils than his soul pitch; wrist-play was not even dross to him; it was an undreamed dream of a dross never met with. Whence this use that was given to him of experience not his? Some force, he dizzily felt, that was not to be judged by our earthly standards, was fighting for him, in him; thoughts of his old cocksure truthfulness made it as if the sun had stood still, or the moon stayed, to back him; he shivered, jam propiore deo, with the fright and delight of a lift from evidence up to inspiration.

Brumby was shaken too; no denying it. The known Pinn soaping him with the known soap of social commerce would have been naught, or else an emetic; this was a Pinn translated, quite a decent human being, Brumby reflected amazedly, not knowing how like dead leaves Nature can make her butterflies, on one side, for their good, and her grubs as green as their pasture, to keep them safe, and her imperilled Pinns provisional replicas of Brumbys. Besides, Pinn, to be fair to him, spoke now with authority, somehow or other, and not even as the mere decent human being, pure and simple; what he said seemed strangely to matter, like the old Roman forecast of victory—words that might have been, in your common adults mouth, mere verbiage; weighty beyond reckoning when a child of three months relinquished the teat to pronounce them, or an ox walked upstairs at the time and jumped out of the first-floor front. Glumness was falling from Brumby; it caked and peeled off him like some old casing of mud in this new sun breaking on the darkness where he had sat among the potsherds.

The nimble spirit that worked in Pinn saw. "Mr. Brumby," he said, "I see you hate praise."

"I know what it is," said Brumby; but half the bitterness of the disillusioned tone was now mere form, a perfunctory ground swell after the real tempest of trouble.

Pinn's wits were so strung up that he all but had humour; a gleam came; before it passed he knew the savour of Brumby's answer for the palate that tells differences. He mastered a happy smile. What a thing it was, this upper hand.

"Just set your teeth, then," he said. "You'll have to bear some, if"—he moved the Warder—"you're going on like this."

"Really, I—" Brumby's tongue, for once, failed; indeed, no words would work, for he stood nowhere long enough to use them; his outworks crumbled; where a guard might have tried to stand at one moment, at the next there was a trickling slope of sand.

Pinn pressed on the good work. "You're the one man, I can see, who doesn't know how you have scored—to my cost, hang you!" O earth, what marvels hast thou seen? He, Pinn, said, "Hang you!" he whose pure lips, even in the stormy March of life, no imprecation had soiled. "Only wish I didn't know it, either!" He said it with the rough, gallant ruefulness of the drubbed boxer giving the drubber his hand; and then, in wonder no longer repressible at the portent of the other's modesty: "My good man, surely you're not deaf. Why, if you had nothing more to go by than"—he checked for one atom of time, gulped down like a dram the rapture of the big throw with the small purse, and then plunged—" than the talk of clubrooms and people in trains and men that you happen to dine with—you must know."

Put it all on, said the wizard tipster at Pinn's ear; likely enough, they have told him his pen is a lump of lead, like yours; still, what matter? As easy to pluck the flower safely from the tallest nettle as from the stumpiest; easier to bleach black white than dye it grey; merely punch a lion in the ribs and he will eat you, but ram your head and shoulders down his throat and you may choke him. "Now by my mother's son, and that's myself, it shall be moon, or star, or what I list"—that is the thing to say to womanish Fate, at noon, and she will soon say, and like saying—"Sun it is not when you say it is not, and the moon changes even as your mind. What you will have it named, even that it is."

Brumby was bluffed. That last, that impossible stroke of bravura undid him. True, he snapped savage fingers. "Club gossip!" he said, " that for it!" But that was only a parting kick to the thought of those others, the sorry few, as they now clearly were, his dispraisers, messing with mud in their poor little backwater, out of the main stream of the great world's opinion—of Hedlum even, that strong and straight mind warped, enfeebled at last, so vain is our human strength. And the rough tone did very well to express rugged modesty.

Pinn took it so. "Eh, but that's like you able men. You win the bays that we poor devils, who haven't it in us, spend our lives trying for, and then it's 'That for 'em I'" Never before had Pinn snapped his fingers, and yet the copy was quite a good snap. "Well, go on. Wear 'em. Snap your fingers at 'em. Gad!"—he said "Gad!"—if I could! I suppose"—and down the scale of feeling he dropped, nobly humble to a mournful resignation—it's try, try, try again for me."

Reassurance was flooding back, a tingling warmth, gratefully stinging, into the Brumby whom frost had so bitten. Like a swan that rude boys have splashed he shook from his plumage the late aspersion; clean again, he mantled proudly; he repaired his beams like the new day. It is a pity not to be able to find figures beautiful enough to match the beauty of this resurrection. He was now so much himself that as he stepped on to the pedestal to which Pinn's hand, itself wonderfully guided, led him, the good fellow felt for the beaten man and wanted to stoop from the height himself had reoccupied, to point out good-naturedly to this poor Pinn, who had certainly owned up like a brick, the graciousness, the balms, the consolation prizes of an honourable licking, so it be taken well. "Come," he replied, quite gently and kindly, " isn't that the best of all?"

Pinn shrugged. "Little to show for it, though," he said. He knew the phrase, the thought, for a low Brumbyism. But when Joshua made as if he were beaten, his pride had to go in his pocket, to take the city of Ai; and who was he, Pinn, to stickle for his? Moral surrenders were one thing, tactical sorties from the fortress of a 'stablished conscience were another. So Pinn issued in force from that fastness, and lo I Brumby nipped in at the gates and hung out a private banner that looked very odd there.

"Does one," he said, with the queerest aping, as Pinn felt, of moral authority, "play the man to have 'something to show for it '?" Brumby was beginning to put vivacity into his performance of Pinn's old part, the man rooted in principle. For the first kind impulse to spread a mattress for Pinn to fall on had received a bracing tonic in the thought that if the mattress were not a good one, Pinn might think twice about falling, or about lying where he fell. Black arts, though scotched, were not killed; the poor wretch might in despair re-invoke Fay unless he could be heartened up to do his duty in that station—Humpty Dumpty's—to which he had now been called.

"Oh, I'm a low beast, I dare say," said Pinn, but not quite so convincingly. It began to feel just a little queer, a little nervous, this manoeuvring outside the old, comfortable moralistic hold.

" I don't say that," said Brumby, leaning over the castle wall, with purpose and circumspection to hand down a modest ration of encouragement to the tactician at his evolutions in the outer dust.

"I may be a low beast," Pinn insisted; his voice had a faint sub-acidity not quite in the part; "but I do own"—it came with an effort—"that it would do me good to have heard it said I could rise to an emergency as—as you've done."

He got it out, with a jolt; the flow was gone. For Pinn the divine accident was over; for Brumby it had begun; the winds of happy inspiration, now failing or spent where Pinn toiled on at his feinting below, blew freshly in upon Brumby's soul posted above on the unaccustomed battlements of goody-goodiness and charmed and pricked to do great things by a sharp, sweet sense of nearness to rosy triumph thorned about with a danger. "Ah!" Brumby's voice put on true sublimity as he washed his hands of the pomps and vanities of a writer's fame, "it's not rising in that sense that matters. Wait till you've tried; you'll agree. My dear sir, it's the act of striving itself, it's the act of going on striving that counts; not the prize. Don't you remember?" And then, for once in his life, Brumby really quoted, not from a previous quoter, but from a book that he had opened the day before, being accidentally left alone in a room with it, and had read with manly contempt, seeing unmistakable signs that its author was Radical, if not sceptical. We all know by heart all that we have ever heard or read. It is only that tackle of various strengths and qualities is needed to fish this or that up from the cellarage. Brumby, worked upon as he was, recited now with scarcely a stumble:

"Great is the facile conqueror;
Yet haply he who, wounded sore,
Breathless, unhorsed, all covered o'er
With blood and sweat.
Sinks foiled, but fighting evermore,
Is greater yet.

"Believe me," he said in a voice that seemed to be all deepening, mellowing chords, "it's not what every one else says that counts; what counts is what you said, that night—that you'd—yes, that you'd write the eyes out of your head before you would put it again in any man's power to do the public another such wrong. Isn't it good to remember it, even now? Won't it be good, twenty, forty years hence, to recall the brave words that will then have moulded your life for so long? There!"—and, in the exaltation of his sense of the necessity, to him, of rectitude in Pinn, he put the hand of a father, almost, on Pinn's stringy deltoid—"come what come may, in the way of name and fame in the world—and trust me, its sweetest is not so sweet, after all—"

The edge of the frame may as well cut down on the picture there; the rest was bathos, flopped into slowly, as the first sprightly runnings of demoniac improvisation tailed off into the dying drip of bad taps. Brumby, the last to inflate, sagged last, but both ended flaccid, and then they trailed home tied to each other, with the wine, that had been such a god in the head, now a sourness on the stomach. Soon they chafed, they wanted to snap; to prevent their sore minds from rubbing each other's skin off they had to keep up a trickle of lubricant verbiage on the place. Pinn was to lunch with a man next day at the Wigwam, Brumby's club. Good! they would meet there. Brumby was lunching there too, with his nephew Dick, expected back in the morning from a holiday. Brumby rather thought Pinn might like the boy. More, Pinn might meet at the club this man Roads who was going to send them all to the workhouse with his new halfpenny paper—to come out, was it next month, or the end of the quarter? "I don't so much fear him," Pinn said, with a ghastly, half-hearted ogle, like a failing septuagenarian flirt's, at Brumby. Brumby's leer back, too, was ghastly enough. The name of the imminent rag—simply, The Paper; it was like the cheapjack's effrontery—grinned at them from the Belton hoardings; each, as he spied on the other's sidelong glance at it, wondered was the tonic still working with which at so sore a sacrifice—so it seemed now—he had tried to brace up a brother's infirmity. Pinn, in whom morality was the more importunate, had a stuck, aghast sense of all he had suffered out there on the bench while that foul man-of-the-world jargon was being pattered by some one no longer definable now except as him, Pinn, simply him. Enough of this self-injury! Things must take their course; no more breaches, whatever happened, in the ring-fence of self-respect.

Pinn went round the whole of that battered paling, inside it, again and again, all the evening, raging at the gap the day's hideous accident had made, and aching for the chance of wherewithal to mend it.

Fortune, he felt, had some bowels left when, latish that night, his chief sub-editor, Dowdon, to whom the tabooing of Fay was not known, just stepped in to say that the critic who was to have noticed the Blumenthal Concert that evening had sent word of illness.

"So, when I found you were not at your house, I sent off the tickets by hand at once to Mr. Moloney's—I felt pretty sure you would wish that done—and the notice has just come in." Poor Dowdon, a Diamond who knew not what he had done, held out some typed sheets. The man was pathetic in his eager and humble hope of praise for promptitude in emergency.

Pinn was not a brute, to bash in the upraised innocent face of that hope. "Thank you," he said, "you did your best in the circumstances." He would tell Dowdon, later, as much as was needed to guard against blunders like this.

Dowdon went out, leaving the notice. Pinn eyeing it where it lay, made a grimace as of nausea, a touch of symbolic action strange in the literal man; then, with a strained, self-forcing impulse, a kind of hard-pumped spontaneity, he jumped up to go for the tongs with which to commit the foul thing to the fire, keeping his fingers unsoiled by its contact. There was a clock over the fire. Could it have stopped? No, it was going. So, then, it was only half-past ten. That concert could not have ended till ten at the earliest. What a journalist that ruffian was!—and, no doubt, quite a long notice, too; Pinn glanced at its length, forgetting the tongs. Yes, nearly a column, just the right length for this, the chief thing of its kind in the year—and the one of which, more than all others, a full review would be looked for in the Stalwart. Competent too, in its way, in all probability; yes, two minutes reading showed that; the sovereign equity of Pinn's mind allowed that the "copy" was perfect. He mused, mournfully:

"'O Hero, what a Hero thou hadst been If half thy outward graces had been placed About thy thoughts and counsels of thy heart.'"

Quoting might not be his line, but that was the run of his thought. And then, again, there came guidance, not the wrecker's flare that had led him at Belton, but this time, he felt, an authentic light of reason's Trinity House. After all, what we must go by is facts, the thing as it is, the act, not the motive—leave God to look after that. Of what use, either, to mix up things different by nature? Politics are politics and music music; a paper's aim should be simply its readers' good, the next day, not the sparing of pain to its editor now, to-night. A course might be galling, and yet be right. With a stern hand he thrust self aside, and initialled the copy.

CHAPTER X

When men are thus combined for their own improvement, or for the good of others, or at least to relax them-selves from the business of the day, by an innocent and cheerful conversation, there may be something very useful in these little institutions and establishments.
ADDISON on Clubs, Spectator, No. 9

The Wigwam Club meets the needs of the man who cares for the things of the mind, but not for the cool soup, with a shining and wrinkling skin, that too often attends them. Politicians may join—Brumby has always loved it—but not as politicians; mere dervishes of party have desolate places of their own to howl in—the Liberal Club and the Halland Carlton. Blood and wealth, if that and no more, lunch at Brett's. For the husks that the ruck of Bohemians do eat you can go to the Four Arts; the Wigwam's subscription winnows away with a powerful fan the painter, musician, or actor, too light in the purse to be quite safe to do with. The club has no billiard-table, no special card-room, even, to tie the straining soul to the earth; only a big dining room and a huge smoke-room, where, just after luncheon, young members feel that now they know what it was like at the Mermaid. Yet the best is loved sanely; the ideal banner floats high, but the fort is reason's; not a wine on the list is really bad, and the boot-boy has a strain of genius; Brumby, who liked to be neat and who had to sit much in the front row on public platforms, with his boots in the reporters' hair, hung, as it were, on the line before the disengaged eyes of thousands, would often wash at the Carlton—the place where you wash at the Carlton is one of the most distinguished in Europe—and then step across to the Wigwam to have his boots polished. Fay called the practice Scriptural. "Moab," he would quote, "is my wash-pot; over Edom will I cast forth my shoe." For Fay had joined the club too, finding that Pinn had not.

In the smoking-room three generations of level business heads and sterling professional men had learnt at first hand from three generations of capable actors, on tour, the blackness of the critics' hearts, and had laid in raw material for talk that has thrilled whole suburbs with delicious shivers of contact with queer, remote worlds, of outlandish brilliancy. In one arm-chair Kelson, the Halland portrait painter, whose too early death was held by many sound judges in the club to have delivered Mr. Sargent from a situation full of menace, had compassed that work of rescue by giving the rein for three years to his preference for green to yellow Chartreuse; from another Bob Burton, the Halland dialect poet, now with Burns, had touched all by the grace of his bow to Fortune's draw in the lottery that lifts one dialect poet—Burns, to go no further—aloft, and depresses another to the dust. You know what a hit was made last spring by Mr. Tom May's Biblical triptych, "Gadarene Demoniacs," shown in New Bond Street in a room devotionally dark, with the dealer's men breaking its message to you in awed whispers and staring if you kept your hat on—a piece reverent in its perception of Gospel truth, yet fully abreast of the van of serious study of insanity; it inspired Father Vernon Baughan, known in the evening Press as the live preacher from Halland, with his almost equally famous sermon on the text—

Let knowledge grow from more to more,
Yet more of reverence in us dwell.

Well, that picture, under its earlier and, as I think, less perfectly happy name of "Lunacy's Progress, or Down a Steep Place," was actually conceived in the Wigwam smoking-room, in talk with Hutton, a young alienist much liked in the club, and Curtin, then manager of the Theatre Royal, who had long thought that more might be done with lime-light to give a haunting quality to the painted eye. In another field Canon Hawkes' book of meditations, The Rock: Some Aids to Limpets, is a part of the Wigwam's gift to English life. Membership was, in Brumby's word, a hallmark; in Hedlum's, a cachet. "Matthew Arnold? Matthew Arnold?" a member once said in reply to another, on 'Change, "I don't think I know Mr. Arnold. Is he a member of the Wigwam Club?"

One of the latest pieces of precious metal to receive this imprint was George Roads, a printer's boy at the Warder office in the last years of Brumby's father, when Early Worm was at his noon of fame as its racing prophet. Roads, with the quick wit of youth, perceived that it was well to send word of the Worm's golden truths, as soon as he saw them in writing each night, to friends of his own, and, through them, to other friends, or clients of theirs, persons in haste to be rich, who could thus put their money on the seer's tips before their issue to the whole world harmfully shortened the odds. A paper pellet dropped from a lavatory window to a partner operating from the footpath was the entire plant of this first modest enterprise. Roads, distrusting human wisdom, backed no horses himself; a tithe of the gains of his friends' friends, when they gained met his few needs, and left so much over that when the leak, as it was coarsely called at the office, was stopped, he set up a tiny tipster's sheet of his own, drew the gifted Worm away from the Warder's service, and had a few thousands put by before a trade rival had the face to give out that the prophet—the man all eyes, as the world thought, on the training-grounds at dawn—had been for some thirty years strictly recumbent in a spinal hospital. Strictly speaking, he had, and so little are the higher kinds of vision understood by the vulgar that Roads' All the Morning Gallops paled from that hour and at last faded from the earth.

It was only now, when, with a head bloody but unbowed under the strokes of brute fate, Roads was thrown back upon thought, that he seized, in all its length, breadth and possible extensions, the fact that the cruel law against gambling was just as full of holes as a net. From the fair and unpolluted flesh of All the Morning Gallops sprang that fragrant violet, the Weekly Eye-Opener, a penny ticket of admission, somewhat swollen with advertisements and the divorces of the week previous, to weekly trials of mental skill in finding out the first letter of its own name. If more than one intellect pierced to the W, the prize fell to him whose envelope was opened first, there being really no surer way of discriminating between the supreme achievement and those others that seemed scarcely lower. Everything Roads touched seemed blessed. In two months the staff of the nearest post-office had to be doubled; in six it was trebled; one short, happy year, and then a jaundiced Government caulked up the hole in the law, and the Weekly Eye-Opener slept with All the morning Gallops.

No weak wailing soiled Roads' lips; he deplored, it is true, an Act which, as he said in his original way, must sap the springs of self-control in the individual; but he would not, like that second-rate person Coriolanus, fight against his cankered country; she was for higher uses. Going on, with £150,000 in pocket, from strength to strength, he founded a daily paper, not for talented people and sportsmen only, but for everybody. Soon he had two—one in a Scotch city, one in an English; each, when opened, undoubtedly gave you a more poignant first sense of the appalling or intoxicating character of yesterday than any of the older journals offered for double the money. You might often think, from the way those niggards fobbed off their customers, that nothing seismic or cataclysmic at all had happened for twenty-four hours. Roads resented this slander on the richness, the diversity of life; no day but, as his paper showed, England was slapped in the face by somebody, somewhere; no day but he rolled up Britannia's sleeve and said: "Feel that biceps!" It kept your blood nicely on the boil. New worlds, too, came in to cover the bald places of the old; and our mother England's broken and precarious flow of murders and connubial convulsions worth reporting was replenished from a score of tributary rills in Paris, Brussels, Vienna and Melbourne; the lusts of New York and the homicides of California enriched for the first time the sacred home life of English families at their next morning's breakfast.

Even then, what vast resources were untapped? Roads' thoughts would rest sometimes with awe and gratitude on the universe's fathomless reserves of spicy copy, or the makings of it—the vernal frailties of Eskimos, the marriage-by-capture of the Khonds, ritualistic amorism in Bengal—none of them yet on the wire; he doted upon them as farmers will dote on rich tracts of virgin soil, not yet touched with the plough, or engineers on unharnessed Niagaras. And why two papers only? Why not others made after their image, enough to dot the whole island, freeze all the old fossils out of the trade, and leave Roads established as the Briton's sole window of outlook on the world?

Halland stood next upon Roads' list for the receipt of this happiness. He had been here six months, equipping an office, priming newsagents, recruiting, as he put it, a smart, live staff; and, lately, dictating the advertisements of the coming birth; they stated frankly how many tons of paper per week would be used, and whence the wood-pulp for it was shipped; the measurements of the piston, driving-wheel and some other salient parts of the engine by which its early edition would be sped to the expectant arms of the extreme north, with a brief memoir of the engine-driver and a very fair portrait of his mother. Everywhere the strong, clear sense of the man, his love of the practical, the concrete, was felt.

The effect on a hard-headed business com-munity was unquestionably great. At the Wigwam Roads was the rage; a Halland lad who had gone forth, as he owned, "on his uppers," he came again with rejoicing, bringing his sheaves with him, in fact holding them out with both hands, and the club rejoiced with him that rejoiced; they found him jannock; loyal clay, he disdained not the pit he was digged from; men liked to sit round him, drawing him out; they called him "Stink o' brass," fondly; and he liked to be drawn; he was great on his dead selves, stepping-stones to the higher things reached since; they were reverently preserved, redecorated, opened to the public, like other relics of the past in good hands.

Roads would make no mystery of the future, either; half his talk was of what to do next; he hoped aloud; peck at it who might, he wore his simple faith on his sleeve, or one even simpler. What some of us see by gleams, or as in a glass, darkly—the tactical uses of guilelessness in a world of over-done guile—he knew through and through. Craft and subtlety he had tried; they were as fine silver; but candour was golden; nothing threw others so thoroughly out of their reckoning; you went ahead with the deal while they puzzled away to make out which lie you were telling, of all that were open. Courtiers and parasites, Roads noticed, constantly fail by refining; they think too well of the prey; old saws, untested by practice, terrorize them, as if every bird that is avian, or human either, were not in a fret to be poking about any net that you set in its sight. "I'm here for what I can get," was Roads' refrain while he "bested" a friend; at such times you would think him the genius of greed, except that he gave you his word for it. "I don't come to town for my health," he would say, as he called you up to be taxed, till you almost wondered if he didn't. It seemed half fun to pay up; at any rate not the ordinary defeat by a pitiful fellow-scrambler; men liked coming in to be sheared that way, and Roads too, from his end of the shears, liked it—not to be rich only, but to king it, to take as if doing a favour, to secure meat with honour. No mere maggot skulking in the cheese, but a first-rate beast of prey, with the world of business for a jungle, he ranged it royally, with a fine, flamboyant, blackguard geniality, at his best, perhaps, when some crew of mediocre rogues would tackle him; then you saw greatness; not merely that he "did them"; he did them blithely, jocundly, jesting and whistling by the way as Cyrano would improvise a ballad while pinking a minor swaggerer.

For all the irons Roads had in the fire, he seemed to have infinite leisure. That is to say, he could organize; he knew that for every definable and recurrent job he had to do he could find a man to do it, not too dear; thus he was everlastingly being set free from piece after piece of the routine work of raking his own winnings in for himself. So, to-day, the morning after the descent of the spirit on Brumby and Pinn at Belton, Roads was one of the first men in at the club. It was scarcely past midday. Hedlum, usually no morning idler in club-rooms, was writing notes at a table by the wall; four devotees were, after a snatched night's sleep, recommencing bridge. Three other men, in arm-chairs, sat on various points of their spines, one eyeing the clock as its big hand slowly rounded to luncheon time, another, cropful from a late breakfast, watching from between closing eyelids the perpetual drift of people on tram-tops across the windows; double windows, with the lower half of each opaque; the seated figures drifted and drifted across as if in space, noiselessly, like fish swimming round and round a glass-sided aquarium, a soundless, mesmeric sight to doze on. The third man was Hewlitt, our friend of the train, now scudding alertly through the papers. Yesterday's talk had quickened his glance at both Warder and Stalwart.

Roads was the man to draw, always; here was the thing to draw him. "Stink o' brass," Hewlitt began inoffensively.

"Sir?" said Roads, undispleased.

"Remembering that you're on your oath, has anything about your destined prey"—a dishevelled Warder and Stalwart were indicated—"struck you of late?"

"Still at it, ain't they?"

"At what?"

"Readying folk to read anything else they can get, to be rid of 'em. Bless you, these old party papers! Party! Good Lord!"

"'Party!' says Burke, 'is—'"

"Burke! I dare say. Some Fenian. Tell you, the thing's played out. Why, look about you; take a business man, average business man. He's got no party; not such a fool. He's fluid, not frozen all up. First this way a bit, then that way a bit—that's him. And d'you tell me he doesn't get up, every morning, fair itching to be rubbed a way no paper in this place has ever rubbed him yet? Kept in touch with—that's what he wants to be."

"What's 'kept in touch with'?"

"Told he's right." Roads' audience grew; his audiences had a way of growing. The bridge-players paused at the end of a rubber. Hedlum, with suspended pen, looked up from his letters, watching the case, with a brief for current morality. The other two men's eyes had already wandered from the clock and the biographed procession of tram-fares. "What would you pay," Roads pursued, with a corresponding rise of voice, "to be told, first thing when you got down to breakfast you were drunk last night, or you revoked, or ate with a knife, or something? That's what they call the game, I s'pose, these party papers. Why, look at the last war. Do folks really want to be told a war's wrong when their blood's up? Or right, a year after, when they're sick of it? That's what they do, between 'em, these papers—blackguard their own customer, turn about; soon as one shift knocks off work at saying the country's a fool, t'other'll come on."

"What if it is though?" said the man of the late breakfast, embittered by conflict with its ingredients. "Half the time," appended Hewlitt, as a loyal Liberal.

"If?" Roads derided. "There's no 'if.' A fool half the time—of course it is. That's Nature. See here." He drew in his chair a few inches, rested his elbows on his knees, and leant forward cogently. " Don't the tide run down half its time? Yes. Nature again. And, take my word you'll soon see every mill in England run with power got out of the tides. And d'you tell me there's any man will say he's above using 'em, except they run only one way? He'll tell the ebb he don't hold with ebbs, will he? Tell the flow its money's dirty, will he? Not a man with a mill. Well—"

"But my dear Stink o' brass," Hewlitt tried to get in.

" Pardon me." Roads, now in spate, whirled away the obstacle. "Ain't there ebb and flow in folks' minds, and high-water marks and low-water marks, and any quantity of tides—tides of sense and pluck and taste and whatever you call it—washing up and down between 'em, fair aching to be put to work?"

"By being—?" Hedlum majestically asked.

He had come nearer.

"Kept in touch with, simply kept in touch with."

"Told they're right, you know," Hewlitt interpreted to Hedlum.

"And why not?" Roads looked round, challenging disapprobation. No one answered for a moment.

When a great positiveness comes along like a train, one retires uncritically to the six-foot way. Perhaps the positive person has really got hold of something; he has momentum anyhow. Hedlum, with a governed, indeterminate smile, and looking as if the whole session were in his charge, waited for some stream of tendency in the general mind to declare itself.

Hewlitt was the first to resume an individuality. " But, my dear chap, some of them!" He shrugged an estimate, thinking of the war days and a Press squealing, in the rear, for the killing of prisoners. Roads turned on him. "Some? Which? If you tell me that any one of them's unclean or common, I say you're not my sort of Christian, and if you wouldn't let it turn a wheel for you I say you shouldn't be in business."

"Yes, yes, my dear sir," said Hedlum cautiously, in his jury-directing voice, kindly and wise, "business is business, we all know, but is it ever really business to make terms with evil?" "Not business? Not?—to bring good out of evil? " Roads broke out into a little blaze of moral fervour that took the colour sadly out of the more mellow beauty of Hedlum's mind. " Now, I'll tell you something. There's towns, English towns, that light the streets with the muck in their dust-holes. That's wrong, is it? Look at the crops on sewage farms—none to touch 'em. That ain't business, ain't it? Do you tell me the rot in people's heads has got to be the only rot that nothing's to be made of?"

"If people were to say, some time," the non-moralizing, speculative voice of Dick came in—like several others he had joined the outer circle round the teacher of practical wisdom—"was it a good thing we gave up acorns?"

"Let 'em," said Roads. But he liked this line less. It made him uneasy, somehow. Only, he would not weaken.

"—or that we took to walking on our hindlegs?" the meditative and unprotesting voice of Dick pursued.

"Where will your paper be then?" cut in Hewlitt, surveying vantage.

"Oh, we'll be there," Roads said, not quite so triumphantly.

"Yelling for the good old diet," Hewlitt laughed. "'Made us the men we are,' hey?"

"It's not so bad, that," Roads allowed.

"'All fours and no affectations'—goodish headline that, hey? "

"You'll see worse," said Roads.

"I was thinking," Dick went on, as if alone with some other fellow-voyager on seas of surmise, "if all the papers said it was a good plan, nearly every one might go and do it."

Roads had recovered. "Eh, but that's like a young man," he said, fathering Dick, "you're all so tall you fear you'll knock the stars right out of the sky if you start moving. Don't mind me; you'll learn; you're not like damned old prigs, the sort this Pinn must be."

From near the door, some thirty feet off, there came the agonized squeak of a chair driven back an inch convulsively on a polished floor. It was five minutes since Pinn, a figure unknown by name to them all, had come in, convoyed by his host Bliss, most innocent of fogies, the Good Goose, as his friends called him, puffing happily as he showed the club of his heart. "Just the two rooms, you see; we're plain people here; just the two rooms and tiny snuggery, across there, for letter-writing, when you need quiet."

"Charming, charming," Pinn had said. Would he make himself at home here for a bare five minutes, while Bliss answered a telephone call in the lobby? Yes, Pinn would write a note, if he might; there was a writing-table near them; he moved towards it.

"Sure you wouldn't rather—?" Bliss had nodded across towards the snuggery door. "No talk, you know, in there, to bother you."

"Sweet human converse, my dear sir, sweet human converse," the lover of man as a whole had answered austerely. " Can any right strain of thought have a worthier obbligato?" The metaphor was a used one of Fay's, without Fay's irony. Pinn forgot this. Feeling nobler for having minted a noble truth, to send Bliss away with, he plunged into his writing, catching nothing articulate from the talkers in the middle of the room until Roads' rising voice stabbed his ear with his own name and that ribaldry. The first furious start of nerves raw before, and now brutally jarred, was not to be helped. But that was all. He drew in his chair, again, quietly. He found he wanted to hear the thing out. He subsided over his blotter.

"Oh, come," Hewlitt had answered. Thank God, Pinn felt, there was one just man in this sink, anyhow. He seemed to know the voice, too, but was not sure.

"D'you defend him?" Roads answered. "D'you defend the stuff he writes?"

"Which stuff he writes?"

"Why, any blessed bit of it. Take to-day's leader, if you like."

"I don't know that that's his."

"Yesterday's? Saturday's? Day before that? Take your choice. D'you mean to say, upon your dying oath, that you can stand a single blessed one of 'em?"

"Albert!" Hewlitt called to a bucolic-looking boy, all chest, haunches and serried buttons, who circulated among the little tables, emptying ash-trays and refolding papers left in disorder. While Albert at Hewlitt's instructions, was fetching a paper from a file kept in a press at the farther end of the room, Hewlitt said: "The fact is, I've not traced, all last week, what I understand to be Pinn's own hand, or his hand at its best. Just listen to this, though." He took from Albert the paper sent for, opened it composedly and folded the leader page to read. "I'll merely read you out the last paragraph of what seems to me simply an average specimen of Pinn's work—no more."

At this moment there was perfect quiet; the words now read out came to Pinn as audible as a jury foreman's to the man in the dock.

"'Enough has been said to leave no doubt as to the nature and the importance of the issue at stake '—"

"Ah," said Hedlum, with a sigh of happy recognition. "Go on; go on."

"'—and we are loath to add even one word that might seem to travel beyond the cardinal question of fact, and in the direction of personalities.'"

"Oh, it's the right way to get agate of slanging anyone, I'm not denying," Roads said, grudging the credit, but also mindful of his own good name as a connoisseur of invective. Hewlitt read on:

"But there is one sign of the times that thoughtful men will not ignore. We could not, whatever we might wish, overlook the evidences of a growing dismay in the enemy's camp—"

"Oh, he's got the turns all right," said Roads, still reluctantly concessive. Hewlitt went on:

"'—in the enemy's camp—or should we say camps?'"

Roads gave a little laugh, less reluctant. "You know, that's rather witty, that bit, with the other lot split up the way they are. ' Enemy's camps '; it ain't so bad, that." He looked round, more generously appreciative. Hedlum's sound sense of humour, too, had kindled at the flash of a sterling, wholesome, recognizable wit. Hewlitt read on:

"'It would be idle to affect blindness to these current proofs that in the opinion of their leaders the game is already up. They labour under an uneasy apprehension of the fact that in their eagerness to secure a tactful success they have been slowly but steadily and at last completely falling out of touch with all that is best in public opinion.'"

"Oh, yes, he has the swing of it," Roads said cordially enough. Hewlitt read on, yet more sonorously. Albert, who now came in, as if to announce something, approached, but waited to speak until the reading should end. As Hewlitt read on, Albert began visibly to listen, his mouth falling open and a foolish smile coming on it, while his body rocked slightly to the lumbering tune of Fay's periods; it was like the luxurious swaying of a pig against the ferrule of the stick you scratch its back with. Roads noticed. The sight of the boy's symptoms confirmed, in its degree, his own gusto for the heavy melody.

"'Absorbed in the satisfaction of perfecting what they believed to be original and effective methods of disparaging the holders of opinions which they do not share, they have insensibly forfeited the respect and regard which our people never fail to pay to any sincere and unselfish endeavour, however ill-conceived or ill-directed, to serve the common good. Mistaking venom of personal attack for argumentative cogency, relying on so-called trends of public opinion which in fact are nothing but the purest figments of the wire-puller's fancy, overrating habitually and deplorably the credulity of a public which, after all, is composed of sane men and Englishmen—'"

"Come, that's the patriotic touch, all right," Roads interjected handsomely. Pinn had turned half round, to hear better. He saw better too, and the sight of Fay's simple medicine working its wonders on those diverse samples of the great public—Hedlum the rounded-off man of the world, mellowly sane as brown wheat, gazing rapt into its shallow and showy moderation as into a mirror; Hewlitt, the sterling party trooper, stirred to his depths by its parade of seriousness;

Albert, the honest yokel, marching in spirit to the tramping, booming trombone music; Roads, the cunning trader, hit between wind and water by the aptness of it all to all these states of the general mind—the sight was a great one, even if you did not know that this moving glove-fit of comment for Lord Albry's speech was but last year's un-worn vesture of the crisis of the misbuilt drain.

But the first bars of a final cadence were audible in Hewlitt's voice:

"'—Englishmen, they have stumbled on through the miry places of latter-day controversy till at last they have plunged over head and ears in a moral slough of their own making. There we leave them.'"

"That's it," Roads said as if in thought, "ease her off and end up tranquil."

"Well?" Hewlitt asked, triumphant, insistent.

"Well," said Roads, "if the man Pinn can keep up to that, his rag may die kicking. I say, though, old man, are you sure that . . . eh?"

"That what?" Hewlitt asked.

"Yo can go oop," Albert broke in, being now disentranced. This was a formula of his, much valued and looked out for in the club since his first arrival some days before, for announcing that a meal was ready.

"What!" said some fine nature, who did not know.

"Yo can start," Albert explained, and went out.

"That's a fresh young savage," Roads said pleasantly.

" Why they ever lassoed him beats me," said the man whose sensibility had received the bruise.

"They did right," Roads rejoined thoughtfully. " The boy's a sample. He's an unspoilt, virgin, country mind. Three weeks ago he was spitting over a bridge with his peers, out there in Arcady—ain't that the word?—of a Sunday afternoon. What fetches him will fetch all rural England."

"You were going to say—" Hewlitt asked.

"About Pinn, you remember?"

"Oh, yes. Are you so sure that it was he that wrote it?"

They were all, except Pinn and Dick, streaming out at the door to go up to lunch, as Roads spoke, and in spite of the happy loosing of tongues as the hungry men drew to their meat, the words were as clear to Pinn, in his seat by the door, as to Hewlitt himself.

CHAPTER XI

Nothing of him that doth fade,
But doth suffer a sea change
Into something rich and strange.
SHAKESPEARE

Dick had something to look up. For he was puzzled; his uncle had not cut him off, this morning, on seeing him back; the reverse. "What! You, my boy!" Brumby had exclaimed with no crack in the fair, round, bellying note that these bonifacial natures emit, even in trouble, at sight of a face they are glad of.

"Yes, I'm back," Dick had said, to the tune of "Let's get it over."

"Good time, eh?"

"Oh, yes," Dick had answered dismissively. That was not it.

"Well, you deserve it. Own up—Oh, I know how you slate your own work, but own up, just for once—didn't it just do you good to read that stuff of yours next day in the paper?

"Mine?"

"'A fine thing, but mine own.'" It was queer how this new way of quoting things, chipping bits off them, or sticking a new bit in, to make them fit, would grow on a man; Brumby winced at the sound of himself as if he had turned a coach-wheel in the street and caught sight of the act in a plate-glass window. "I refer, of course, to your exceedingly scholarly and discriminating critique of the Mountain Painters' Exhibition," he added, heading back to the safe, sound old jargon of the business.

Dick gaped. "Read it? In the paper?"

His uncle laid on Dick's shoulder the hand of an approbation only the warmer. "Able and modest too! Quite right! Dick"—he massaged the praise into the reluctant shoulder with a firm, feeling grasp—"it was a first-rate job you made of it—the first quite first-rate job you've made of anything."

Dick's mind jumped across and back between conceivable explanations; none did to stand on for long. "Why, how on earth," he asked, perching on one for an instant, "did you come to see it, sir?"

"It's a free country, Dick. Editors, even, may read their own papers. There, there, blush but hear me—"

Mountebanking again with the words! A twinge traversed him. He steadied. "Seriously, my dear boy, that notice was as thoroughly balanced, as mature in judgment, as competent in point both of technical knowledge and of literary finish as"—the emphasis soared up climactically—"as the work of many an old journalistic hand."

"Uncle—" Dick began, to no purpose. He was silenced, bundled out good-humouredly; Brumby was busy; Dick had better cool his bashfulness outside; or, let Dick go on ahead to the club and not put off luncheon if Brumby were late; perhaps he might not come at all; he was frightfully busy.

So Dick, alone in the big club-room with the unknown Pinn, bade the boy fetch the Warder of Wednesday week, when the birth-strangled babe should have lived; and Pinn, as he heard the order to Albert, wondered had no one in Halland any-thing left to do but to keep that day's paper scraping and grating in contrast against all the ones that had followed.

When the paper came, Dick found the place, read a line, marvelled, read a few more, and knew all about it. How could he not? Fay had tumbled out under his nose, that night, this dustcart's load of old rags; Dick knew at once the tags that lay uppermost. So it was Fay's comedy; Fay that had cast him for the part of the goose that the clown rescued. Dick had he not been Dick, might have raged; had he been yet more un-Dick-like, he might have been touched. Neither feeling came; only, at first, a finished idea of his uncle, the master journalist, the expert, the public's analyst, for whom this refuse of Fay's was pure gold. Not that Dick saw any sin in it all; rather, a strange way of going without what had savour, like giving up salt. To fit word on thought—no; to say this made two things of them—but to hold the thought, to force it up and up the scale of clarity to where it and some unsought word rushed together and a new thing came to life, as when Adam first spoke—to Dick this was the great, the one game; the gift of speech might have only come in last night; there he was, at his first day's fun with it, wild in love with all that the living, limitless thing might work out to.

Had you, who so love the drama, come on the cook, at her fell work, who burnt seven of Massinger's plays, the only copies, leaf by leaf, as shields to pie-crust, Dick's thought might be clearer to you. Of course he had seen speech dead before; the corpse lies about, in everyone's sight; pathetically, in the mouths of tongue-jaded townmen wearily simulating life with pitiful little stocks of faded slang and tenth-hand repartee; sluttishly, on the lips of modish people straining to do more than justice to their own affinities to rodents; and again, embalmed and lying in state, ghastlily, with crowds gaping in rapture at the bowelless carcass, in that grisly histrionic business of the posturer Albry. But with Dick it had passed as a thing of course that in chaff and in politics words were used not as themselves but as something less, as you might use cricket-bats for lighting fires, or train sweet-peas up fly-rods. Not till now had he seen with eyes fully open, the rite of splashing solemnly about in a vocabulary, for splashing's sake, the preference for just jingling, for the sound they made, the bunch of keys that, rightly turned in the locks, were inlets to gardens by rivers in Bagdad. And the strangest thing of all was connoisseurship in the practice; to a man like his uncle there were, it would seem, a better and a worse in the tread of making words stand for nothing; there were qualities of nullity, degrees of skill in keeping mind and heart blank; the void was not all one, nor zero a level.

How far did it spread? He wondered. After all, might not his uncle be, in his dealer's way, right? Was Fay's patter of symbols, symbolizing nothing, what people, perhaps, really wanted, what more and more people were coming to want till at last the whole art of significant speech might atrophy clean away, out of men's minds, like an unused muscle, words growing more and more voluble, each of them counting for less, till we worked clean round the circle and sat again chattering on the trees, with a Roads to say we were right? Or was his uncle a gull, a freak, at whom every one laughed? Had the painters of those pictures laughed, when they read? Or did they too—?

In the midday hours that room was like a foreshore; swift rising tides of tweed and broad-cloth would flood out at one moment over its vacant stretches of bulging and puckered red leather, till nothing was bare, and again some ebb—the hour for luncheon, the hour for return to business—would leave all high and dry, and the foreshore only littered with the leavings of the receded bore—tobacco-ashes, used matches, scrunched-up envelopes. One such tide you have seen, and the setting in, at Albert's potent word, of an ebb; the only major deposits of the spent flood had been Dick and Pinn; then Bliss had come back and cleared off Pinn, and now, so long had Dick mused, the tide was making again; the vanguard of the fed dropped in, using toothpicks, or cutting cigars, and sank plump on the red cushions, ordering coffees and curacjoas.

One group, flown with insolence and luncheon and abounding in a happy consciousness of their most jannock selves, came chaffing an image of good-humour in its midst, a German of caricature, a musician of the comic papers, and yet an authentic German and a rare musician, and a Samson seasoned to the job of making sport for Philistines at odd times, content enough that the poor things, shut out from life, should have consolations.

"What about your Kaiser, now," one of them was asking, "cheeking England that way about Waterloo?"

"I tell you fott, my boy," was the emphatic answer, "we must strengzen our Navy."

There were roars of laughter, derisive shouts of "We!" "Who's 'we'?" Wigwam badinage was robust.

"My dear men," began Hewlitt, "Blumenthal's quite right. He—"

"Go it, Hewlitt! Good old Radical! Back the foreigner," cut in some purer patriot.

"Foreigner!" cried Blumenthal. "Me zat's naturalized!"

"Since when, my friend?" asked the patriot sweetly.

"Since breakfast-time, eh, Bloomer?" another rapier clinked in. "Didn't you just read that puff of your show in the Stalwart this morning and then go off and turn Englishman straight in honour of Albion's Press?"

"Albion's! The anti-British rag!" the patriot muttered. But in this place party was nothing, wit's cut-and-thrust everything, so he forebore. "How much a time does the Stalwart rush you, for puffs that size?" was all that the brilliant fellow said out.

"Belief me, my friends," said Blumenthal, "I haf already not seen to-day zis so famous critique of my concert of last evening."

All remonstrated in one breath. "Blumenthal! Blumenthal!" "Bloomer, be good." "Oh, fie!" "It was last night he read it!" "No, he only wrote it."

"Dear Bloomer is so modest," Roads said, "that he never will see it unless—"

"Make him!" "Read it him by force!" "Let's hold him down," was shouted by one and another, and so the meat-fed wits concerted a eupeptic lark, sitting in a ring, with the German set in the midst, in a big, soft chair; from his throne he beamed on the children at their play, his little lathe-turned legs dangling clear of the floor. Roads fell into place as president of the session—a way of his at such times; he would melt into the chair, in a kind of vapour, to re-condense there into a Roads. Blumenthal, primed by him with a cigar and a meetly laced coffee—even the guiltiest, Roads said, must not perish of want in the hands of justice—sat back god-like whole and round, pleased with the innocence of mankind.

"Now, gentlemen," he said, "as our Shakespeare says, 'I am armed and well prepared.'"

There was the stock roar at his conscious Englishness. As it died down, the reciting drone of the voice of Hewlitt, chosen off-hand for this liturgy, drifted across to petrify Dick:

"'When Dr. Blumenthal conducts a passage of Wagner like this, it is as if the hearer turned a corner at some primal dawn and lit upon God, making the earth—'"

Interjections of " Oh! Oh!"—"I say, though!" "Beastly casual—coming on God like that!" were stilled by Hedlum's deliverance, "The words, if I may venture to say so, seem to me singularly apt." Then the rest first knew, what Hedlum's instinct had known before, that it was just what they had been going to think. "So," assented Blumenthal, from the full heart. There was a quick laugh again. "Apt to me?

No, but to Wagner, whom I, even I, cannot disable! Yes!"

"Apt, I was trying to say," Hedlum resumed, clement to man's incorrigible vice of interrupting, "to the vague but profound and vast suggestive-ness of great music."

"So," assented Blumenthal; "Hewlitt, you can already strike me again. Ze stripes are goot."

Hewlitt read on, to a deepening ring of hearers, Brumby, who had just come in, amongst them.

"'You stand, if only one instant, in Creation's forge; your very body shakes with the fall of the hammer that beats out the half-made world.'"

The ring, as a whole, were rather impressed. "A very fair appreciation," one enthusiast ejaculated. "'Divinely fair,'" a still unmoved scoffer quoted, "'and most divinely tall.'"

"Tall!" cried the musician. "For Wagner! Zis praise tall! No, a tousand times!"

"What on earth has it to do with Wagner?" Dick intervened, speaking as if alone with one person, but with a first tang of bewildered indignation in his voice, breaking in on its childlike want-to-know quality.

"So? No?" Blumenthal was polite, though scandalized. "Wiz Wagner, no? Wiz whom, zen, in zis wide world of music?" His gesture was vast, circumferential.

For the moment perplexity closed again over Dick's head. "Music!" was all he said. Hedlum, having eyed him with the temperate contempt due from a good man to the cutter of a poor figure, nodded to Hewlitt. " Had you not better proceed?" he said, doffing and wiping his spectacles restfully. "Perhaps the junior member of the club will set us right when you're done." Blumenthal, softer-hearted, leant over towards Dick, in fatherly pardon of the blasphemy. " When you are old," he said kindly, "you will, as me, feel in zese words fat and juicy meaning."

The reading went on. Dick, semi-dazed, watched the exhumation, from this inexplicable grave, of his own naked, new-born babe, so private and tragic to him. Limb by limb, it came out, indecently successful with these deluded savages. Now:

"'It is to stand at night on a hill, till something gives—some bolt that has barred you out from reality breaks in your mind, and you feel with your body the roll of the earth, and the wind of the rushing through space, past other stars.'"

And again, in some mad context:

"'It almost brings to the face the sting of the blown granules of ice, on a high pass at dawn.'"

"And now," Hewlitt said as the recital closed, with a gesture of ceding to Dick the general ear, "the man who knows will—"

"Who else *should* know?" Dick began with his blundering reliance on realities.

There was a great laugh. As a butt, Dick was ousting the German. "Who, indeed?" asked Hedlum, placidly fondling his jest, "but the youngest among us?" "'A child shall lead them,'" some Biblicist quoted.

Dick was struck. What use, after all, to explain, where he could explain so little? "I'm sorry, sir, you should be hoaxed," he said to Blumenthal.

Hewlitt fired at the word. "Hoaxed!" he said hotly; he thrust the open *Stalwart* on Dick. "Be so good as to look at that." Dick looked at the notice blankly. The ring was now melting away, partly in mercy to him. "Do try," Hewlitt said improvingly, "to have a little imagination. For one thing perhaps you may come to conceive what Art means. For another perhaps you'll conceive we're not all undergraduates here; in this club, as it happens, we don't play off hoaxes."

"Why, it's a regular theft," Dick was muttering, to himself mostly.

"What—to disagree with youth?" laughed the patriot Bunce. "Flat burglary. Good! It always was."

"Theft, I mean, literally," Dick said, half attending, while half of him held off and thought.

Brumby came forward. "My jurisdiction, Bunce," he said. They were friends. Bunce, nodding, went out. Every one went; chambers and offices called to them. Brumby, alone with Dick in the residuary reek of smoke, smells of drinks, and used breath, put the hand of a kind and wise condescension again on Dick's shoulder and said in reminiscent, humorous reproach, "Literally, Dick, my boy? Literally?" Brumby at all times talked as hacks write up the text to go with a picture—the "letterpress." First came the vision of himself, rightly posed; then fit words for the hero, afterwards. What he saw now was a commanding officer, a scarred veteran, handsome, patient and melancholy, once stupidly insulted by the last-joined subaltern—and now the headstrong boy had tumbled into the very lapse his folly had thought to upbraid in a Belisarius, a Bayard, a Colonel Newcome. "Dick, my boy," said these heroes, with a touch of whimsical, long-suffering playfulness, "literally?" Dick, plague take him, would never fall into his place in heroic compositions. "You heard," he said, just as if no tableau were in hand, "the stuff he read?"

"Yes, yes," said Brumby, stretching a point of forbearance at the crass interruption.

"I wrote that—whole blocks of that."

"Dick, Dick, my dear boy."

"I wrote that." Dick's stress, quitting the first word, came down hard on the second.

" Dick, what's the matter with you? Last night you were in Cumberland."

"Of course, but " Dick's gesture tried to brush Brumby away.

"But, but, but," Brumby's voice came again like a groom's buzz round a touchy horse; " you don't write on music, eh, Dick?"

"Good Lord, no! But—"

"Nor for the Stalwart—eh, Dick? No, no; only one traitor in the dear old camp."

"There is a traitor?" Dick snapped at the word. " Why, he did it then."

"Yes, yes, no doubt, no doubt." While he spoke, like a nurse droning fretful infancy into quiet, Brumby put out the soothing hand again.

Dick, with a twitch of distaste, subtracted his shoulder. " Uncle, I'm not drunk. That night—the last I was at work—I wrote that rant. I wrote it about those pictures."

Then Brumby did, for a silent instant, peer into the well and saw, not indeed the whole dripping figure of Truth, but a first tab or loop of her wet raiment. "D'you mean," he said, working it out piece by piece, "it was not you wrote that other—the notice of that exhibition of pictures?"

"The slops that the Warder printed?"

"Slops!" The master craftsman was outraged. "A first-rate piece of journalism." Even as he gave worth its due, he turned; he saw something move in the well. "Why, who the deuce, then, did write ours?"

The question, asked chiefly of the ambient air, was answered by Dick. "That Irish ape, of course."

"Why d'ycm say that?"

"He spilt it out, pails of it, one time I stuck."

"You stuck, did you? Oh?" Brumby was grim. So his own flesh and blood had been failing again, and Fay had rescued the paper. Fay had kept the coach going. "You stuck, again?"

"It all ran into knots, what I thought of saying; two or three small things I wanted to write down more and more just as I meant them wouldn't come right, and the rest was a thin flux of piffle; and the time was going. Fay saw. He was decent enough in his own thief's way—gabbled some rot I might pass off instead of a notice—the rot that's in," Dick explained, with a spurning flick of his boot at the old Warder dropped on the floor.

"Oh, you did let him give you a lift with it, then?"

"My good sir!" Dick exclaimed, getting red. It was rude, but in Dick the ferocious self-respect of youth had not yet been broken to harness.

No condign reprimand followed. You cannot, the while you stand on your dignity, also lie flat on your stomach, peering down into a well.

"What did you do, then?" asked Brumby, who might have consumed Dick with fire so nicely, had fortune been kinder.

"I tried on, a bit; it wouldn't go; so then I chucked it."

"But the stuff that you'd written?"

"I threw it in the fire."

"In the fire—literally, my exact friend?"

"Well—at it."

"It seems it didn't hit." Brumby paused, inferring, piecing out. Then he spoke slowly, with strain, each word a painful inch of ground, you would say, won by the higher equities of the soul from interest and inclination. " And Fay took the pains to save it, and, I dare say, thought, rightly or wrongly, he was not charging too dear in accepting a cast-off shred of botched work from the ash-heap, as some small set-off to the first-rate thing he was giving, freely, to the paper in its hour of need. 'Pon my word, what he did was almost excusable."

"You mean—to palm off what I'd said of pictures one day as what he thought of music another?"

"My dear boy, it's easy for you and me, if we merely care to be smart, to make out a fine case against him, but isn't the vital question this—has any substantial injustice been done?"

"To the pictures he hadn't so much as given a look at?"

"Come, come, he's bad enough, God knows—don't I know it too, to my cost? Still, let's be fair, Dick. Fiat justitia, mat coelum—eh? You see," the ripe senior went on, in russet, richly autumnal tones of garnered sense and sane charity, "I'm afraid it is out of the question, with men what they are, to make a paper's assessment of the merits of various works of art as purely impersonal as you or I might wish."

Dick shuddered. Criticism impersonal! Brumby went on, from increasing heights: " Meanwhile, in any merely personal, merely individual valuation of such things, there must always be an element of—well, of uncertainty; so that, for all we know—though, of course, I'm with you on the general question, Dick, I'm with you on that—in the special case of the Warder's criticism of these artists the presence of that element, that alloy as I may say, cannot without inexactness be wholly attributed to Fay's unfamiliarity —due, as this was, to an emergency—with the actual details of particular paintings; nay, to be quite honest, which of us can say for certain that this element was appreciably in-creased by it? Sympathy, remember, and insight and experience can do much; and then, no doubt he would feel doubly bound, in a case of this kind, to exercise sobriety and moderation and breadth and catholicity of judgment; and these, when you come to think of it, are, surely, the most essential, the only absolutely and invariably essential parts of a critic's equipment."

"I don't follow you, uncle," was all Dick could say at the moment. Now that he had the use of his eyes, with the bandage of respect off, it took his break away to see the moth-eaten shoddy of tins mind unrolling its rotten folds.

"You will, my boy, all in good time. Youth judges harshly. But as to Pinn—!"

"Pinn?" Dick stared.

"You don't know! Oh, of course. Now that's a traitor for you. And, by George," said the man, master of himself, remembering suddenly, "he's upstairs now. I saw Bliss and him washing—and now why the deuce can't they finish their guzzling? Ah—!"

Belief in the efficacy of invocation was supported by the sight of Bliss and Pinn politely struggling for posteriority through the swing-door.

CHAPTER XII

The prophets prophesy falsely; and the priests bear rule by their means; and my people love to have it so; and what will ye do in the end thereof?
JEREMIAH v. 31

If A be really for having it out with B out it comes; let the wish only burn with due heat of its own, and any small hamperings of time, place and usage will dry off duly from round it, much as the swaddling sheaths parch down to nothing from under the bursting flame of a poppy. In a few minutes Bliss, from a fond, expansive host, had first decreased mystically into a detail and then diminished clean out of the room; Dick, though a more impracticable solid, had declined into a disconnected dark object projected on a middle distance of red leather, and Brumby was opening the snuggery to Pinn, to minister to him, there, a helping of those sweets of human converse for which Pinn had forgone earlier acquaintance with the peace of that interior.

"Mr. Pinn, a breach of faith—" the honest, rugged fellow began, the grammatical subject tumbling out, like a cry, without thought for its predicate.

"Sir!" Pinn's voice beat to quarters. Were boarders coming?

"I may say, a fraud of a gross type has—"

"Sir!" said Pinn again, with no art, rushing half out of his guard; the guilt of last night made him jumpy on his stance.

Brumby saw, and cooled; so Pinn was cracking, perhaps nearly done with; "—has been practised upon you," said Brumby, the last words slowly, with malice and gusto, to note how they set Pinn trying to wriggle invisibly back to the ground he had quitted in panic. "On Tuesday night—a fornight ago—" Brumby went on, slowly, watching.

" Yes?" said Pinn, itching for speech.

"That night," Brumby retailed the words, "my nephew, whom I have just introduced to you, wrote, in my office, for use in the next day's Warder, a notice of the Mountain Painters' Exhibition. It did not appear in the next day's Warder. It does appear in the Stalwart to-day."

Hope jumped up, a flicker of light, from the ashes of Pinn's suffering complexion. "I beg pardon, but, surely some strange misunderstanding   If I remember rightly there is no notice of that, or, indeed, of any picture exhibition in to-day's Stalwart."

"The missing copy," Brumby went on with crushing, massive levelness of tone, "appears in the Stalwart as a notice of a concert."

"Good heavens! Good heavens!" Pinn's genuine start at coming on this novel cantrip of Fay's was the making of his demeanour as a piece of fence. A little stunned, in good truth, by the news, and travelling with conjecture, he felt the next instant the tactical value of what had not itself been tactical. Not by design, he had got the right key; now, to compose in it. " Mr. Brumby," he said in the same shocked voice, "for the wrong done to you I'm, you'll believe me "

"Oh, we all do wrong, now and again." The robust Christian, thinking for one wild moment that Pinn was making a clean breast, relaxed. Take this little bonus in advance, he seemed to say, on any frankness I shall find in your confession. Vain hope! No confession was coming; censure, rather; a look of protest, aghast.

"What!" said Pinn. "You'd let him off!"

"Him?"

"The thief!" The receiver almost shrieked. "The thief of your valuable property!"

"Oh, our loss—as to that—" Brumby shrugged a modest valuation of Dick's labours. In this commerce of deceits naked sincerity rose now and then to a moment's commercial value, and then again was submerged.

But Pinn's altruistic indignation went on nosing away at the business—one end of the business, waxing and turgescent at each injury to Brumby that it explored. "Rob you of what was vital to your next day's paper! Why he stopped, his eye took light; it revolved as if seeking a file of the Warder—"you can have had no notice next day of that important exhibition."

"We made shift, you know. One does, you know," Brumby said hurriedly. Him, too, furtive panic re-invaded. Pinn, thanks be, made no move filewards. "That's over, anyhow," said Brumby, on a freer breath. "You mustn't mind about me; I've stood worse. But that this thief, whoever he is it was too bold this; their eyes met; each saw that the other was scouting—"should palm the loot off upon you, for what he did—by gad, sir, it was abominable!"

Each spy caught the eye of the other, and saw his game, and saw too that his own game was seen, and yet drove on with it, partly because he could not cut clear if he would, partly from some last drain of hope; both were in the cheat's last lap now, the dead weariness of playing tricks, the sick longing not to be so low, but to bring off just one grand haul of rogue's gains, enough to set them up again for good as honest men. Like the clerk who has filched an odd fiver per week for some months, each burned, with a thirst that seemed very like the true thirst after righteousness, to wipe out all his nasty little moral soilures, or his lacks of sportsmanship, with the sponge of one big deal which, put through in the right way, would see him safe back to solvent rectitude, at ease to make his peace quietly with men, or at any rate with the gods, for whatever fell short of the ideal in the mode of his salvation. "Oh, we won't talk of that," Pinn's voice dragged on dully, a sound as of tired, shuffling feet that must still mark time in dust, dust; "the Stalwart's back is fairly broad. It's your case I'm thinking of. And if you do find out the thief and care to—to press the matter—say, to prosecute, then of course anything I can do—Ah, Bliss, you back!"

Bliss, happily fussy as the tug that berths a liner, was leading in Hewlitt. They had left together, it seemed, and Bliss, as they went along, had said something of Pinn's being there, and Hewlitt had stopped dead; they must go back; he wanted an introduction. "Fact is, Mr. Pinn," he explained, "I am a joint honorary secretary of the National Progressive Union, and I want your leave to reprint as a leaflet that most telling leader—if it's not impertinent to say so—that you gave us in the Stalwart last, last—"

"Yes?" Pinn almost begged, as again a tiny tongue of that flame licked up out of the ashes.

"Last—oh, no—Wednesday—a fortnight ago," said Hewlitt, and the flame went out.

Brumby, drawn off a little for manners' sake, sucked every word into thirsting ears. So, too, did Fay, now in the large room. It was Fay's club hour; at dead low-water of each day's life of the club he would slip in and rush through the papers. Pinn saw him talking with Dick, and looked at Brumby's face again and saw more foul play there. But Hewlitt had to be answered.

"May—?" said Pinn. "Oh, will it do if I let you know later?"

Hewlitt was sorry; he hated to pester; only, they must go to press at once, and the thing was so good, and really no voter in all Halland should go without reading it. A silence followed, silence, not as that of the grave, for that is rest from sound; this was an ache for it, a hungering sense of stretched strings and expectant tympani. Fay, weakly merciful, ruffled a Field to temper for Pinn that agony of importunate stillness. Hewlitt half turned from the patient. "Brumby," he said, "can't you help me? Forget you're a

Tory. Persuade him. If you were the Junius, and I were—if I were the Primrose League, now wouldn't you give me your leave?"

"In most cases," began Brumby, "no doubt." Then he stopped. Let the humbug get out of the hole himself, if he could, he that digged in the dark to trip others.

"You make reservations?" said Hewlitt. " Jealousy, thy name is journalist. Fay, now, you'll have no bias; speak up for me."

Fay looked up, sheepish and deprecant, wincing for Finn's distress while tickled with the humour of it. Bliss seconded the playful appeal. "Come along, Fay," he called genially, "help press a wider fame on a blushing author."

Fay shambled nearer. Pinn the blushing author, Pinn the bushel-covered light, Finn the violet 'neath a mossy stone—the idea sustained the Irishman; his breed feed on such moon-dews; they pick proteids from these humours. Still, he had pity "for all souls in trouble, here or in hell." "Well, personally—" he began.

It was his way, they knew. "Yes, yes," Hewlitt pressed, "we know—you're not an author yourself, and all that"—and, in fact, Fay had helped that to be thought—"but if you were? Suppose, just suppose, it were you that had written that smashing—"

"I mean," stammered Fay, " that, before I—"

"Before you'll say, you'll sink into the earth—is that it?" Hewlitt chafed. These diffident people were maddening.

"I mean, just now, before I—well, before came in, I saw Hedlum—"

"If he'd seen you, now," sniffed Hewlitt.

"—brushing your hat, with his coat on," Fay mildly concluded.

"Lord!" cried the politician; postponing the national interest, he rushed from the room, in his own. Bliss, whose hats were studies, nervously followed; none would be safe, with the short-sighted man in the lobby. Pinn hung for a second inactive, till Fay, with a quick little stamp of impatience, pointed him back to the snuggery door whence they had all been debouching into the outer sea of club carpet. Then, with a low "Thank you," breathed from the heart, Pinn went to earth without further formality.

Brumby, too, speeding outwards through the swing-door, found time, as he passed Fay, to growl, with the full gruffness of an unflattering Briton's hard-won admiration, "You've gumption, anyway."

Fay and Dick only were left, Fay wrigglesome all over. No inch of skin but seemed to be dodging an apprehended dart from Dick's quiver of killing simplicities. Dick marvelled. He asked, "Was that a trick, too?"

"The hat trick? Looks like it. It got 'em out, all three, at any rate."

"But why?"

"The man was wretched." Fay glanced at Pinn's refuge. Hewlitt came in as he spoke. "In time, I trust," said Fay, to him, anxiously. ' "Yes, many thanks; the crisis was past, some one had pulled him off it, no doubt. Finn gone?"

"You didn't pass him in the hall? " said Fay with surprise.

"Going, was he? I must give chase."

"You know the short cut to his office?"

"The slummy way?"

"By Hanging Gate."

"I know."

Hewlitt was gone. "Another!" said Dick, and marvelled. "I say, though," he added.

"Yes?"

"About that stuff you wrote, the picture stuff; you—knew all right what rot it was?"

"My dear boy—" began Fay placably.

Dick plunged on.

"It was just fooling, wasn't it? You don't believe in it?—no, of course you don't, like these old geese—my uncle, and all of 'em in this place—everybody else outside it too. I dare say, barring you; it's just for some sort of game you patter off that hash of lies, don't you? These people here have the lie right in their souls—if their brains were only shamming dead, like you, there'd be hope; but they ain't; they're carrion and like it—death's life to 'em; they don't want what's real; it's too sharp air for 'em; they couldn't breathe it; and you, that do the lying for 'em—there's no one else but you that knows or cares a hang what it means to see things for oneself and to get your own feel of them."

Fay waited a moment; Dick breathed.

"What was it like now, there at the pictures?" Fay asked, at first shyly; then, with a rush, "Now, wasn't it just bursting, all a-tingle, into a June world at dawn?"

"I knew you knew," said Dick.

"A first dawn of all, it would be like, rising, not on the dust of any old days?"

"Yes, yes," Dick asserted, "on it, over it, shining and wet, like some immense pity, opening pitiful eyes. Yes," he pressed Fay; they might have been arguing for hours; "yes. Yes."

"Faith, how should I know?" Shyness, scared at her own lifted veil, was letting it fall again.

"You do. You're the only one does. There's no one to talk to, but you. You do know."

"I did, you might say." The veil was forgotten at the other's call for company in a loneliness. "I was right in the garden, once on a time, and then I played at making flaming swords and then—well, I was turned out with them."

"Swords?"

"Lies, you know. I took to the lying—not for fun, you know, exactly—we were nesting then, my wife and I, and the rations don't come in now for young ravens in the way they used to do in Syria—and then there's some plaguy way the soul works, so that you can't see truth if you give up telling it. 'Your young men shall see visions '—is that how it goes?—'and your old men shall dream dreams'; it's a white hair, every lie; you grow old in them. Ah, but the fine things I've seen, like you, and now I can doze and dream of 'em. I remembered, when reading your copy. Dead true it was—that I could tell still—news of a real thing that had come in the way of a real being."

"Tumbling about among pictures—yes; but music! My dear chap!"

"Why not? It does say, at least, what had happened to somebody, somewhere. If I'd written, my stuff would have told what had happened to nobody, nowhere. Pinn, or some vice-Pinn of his, sent round for some copy, so I pulled this about and threaded it on to a sort of a string that we use in the trade, and threw in a corpse of a phrase here and there, to make corpses like Pinn feel at home with it." Three yards away a tossed Stalwart lay on the floor; the tall heading, "Blumenthal Concert," was legible.

"Why," said Fay, the wild man in him shying again, restive under these intimacies, "why it looks like the real thing, just, from here."

"'See large,' as Sir Joshua says. Now, see." Dick grew grumpy and clumsy. "Your game's up, isn't it? Oh!"

Dick half turned at a creak from the snuggery door; not in time, though, to see Pinn's face protrude warily, dwell for a hungry instant on Fay, then, blackly, on Dick, and vanish again. Fay saw; he saw everything. "You're sacked," Dick resumed, "I too, perhaps, for of course I must have it all out with my uncle; only, unless he does sack me, I'll stick on a while and take soundings, to see if there's bottom at all, or whether the whole Press goes down all the way to some central waters of falsity under the earth."

"'M? Metaphors—mind them. They're all right; only, mind them."

But the senior workman failed to head off the apprentice. "You've seen fit to go halves in my copy," said Dick, labouring to be brutal, "so you've got to go halves in the pay. It's your own confounded fault."

"Sir!" Fay stiffened and reddened. As he did, the swing door whined on its hinge; another head, Brumby's poked in, coveted Fay, and was gone. Him, too, had Fay seen, as his way was; and Dick had not, as was his. The rigidity thawed out of Fay. "You say, while one's out of work, the other—either—whichever it be—is to share with him?"

"You'd like it that way?" said Dick, kicking himself in spirit. Lout, why had he not put it that way himself?

"You agree?" Fay was pressing.

"Well—seems reasonable."

" You agree?"

"Oh, yes."

"So do I."

CHAPTER XIII

I am cast upon a horrible, desolate island.
DEFOE, Robinson Crusoe

The Fays dwelt in an inner suburb, now rotting, built sixty years before to meet the needs of refined minds. Every bell-pull traversed the diameter of an Ionic column; not a brick, except, of course, in the backyards, peeped from under the long, classic robe of stucco, biennially painted, in the old days, an almost Parian white, to keep up in the colour the spirit of the form. Now it was painted no more; landlords themselves, in a changed world, had lost faith in the power of beauty over the mind, and the quarter's chaste visage yellowed towards the grave, pencilled on the flat parts by rude boys and freely lined at each accessible protuberance by passing strikers of matches. On the moist majority of days the stucco sweated a million dirty pearls, and in summer it curled and peeled peacefully off in the sun, like Giotto's frescoes at Assisi. In the gardens the grass under the leggy hollies and privets had mange or had died, every blade, of the black death, but a roughly compensatory herbage sprouted among the powdered glass between the setts of Fay's street, a blind alley with one corner of its estuary turned by a slattern newsvendor's shop window, full of fly-blown novelettes, dress-making journals, and sunken tarts; the other by the dusty, many-bottled windows of a "grocer's licence."

Here the Fay's had camped at their first landing on the island, with a single eye to a cheap shelter from the weather and the aborigines, as the castaway in other wilds, when he chooses his hole in the rocks, or his hollow tree, only asks which will keep off the beasts and the rain, with least done to it. That the quarter mouldered was good; neighbours were possibilities of molestation to ferocious shyness; those who might call and those who would not differed as a noxious from a negligible fauna. Here mildew and cobwebs, the burst paint-blisters and straddling weeds gave every hope that society too, in the sinister sense, had rusted down to harmlessness. From the cave, the stockade, they would issue to buy from the natives; for some they even conceived a kind of regard, the explorer's for the "friendlies"; a stranger civil in the tram or a greengrocer who had missed a chance to overcharge would be distinguished cordially in talk that night, as one commemorates singular concessions from Afghans or finenesses of nature in horned cattle, God help them.

The furniture fitted the house, in a way—every stick of it picked up at auction, by some one whose fingers, working in the agonies of selection, or of bidding, could feel each other through the purse; picked, not for its looks, not to sort with the rest, nor because some one else had the like, but just for its power to serve some primary need, to sit or lie on, or to keep clothes from the moth, or sugar from

Jemmy. "What a featureless jumble," you might have said, wrongly, at sight of the deal and maple, oak and mahogany and ash, that took so little thought to set one another off. Rightly seen, with every attribute ignored that has not existed for the creating sense of the collectors, the whole had a quite tense unity of character, each piece of it driving straight at the one seen end, as plain things do in rude places where the yoke and milking-stool are spare and purposeful, with a set leanness of utility like that of athletes; only, there, the taking of the nearest means to the plain end is seen; it hits the eye. Here, at the Fay's, the strictness of fitness in chair and wardrobe was spiritual, resting on the user's habit of paring his own idea of them down to that of naked servers of first purposes and leaving out of consciousness every clogging irrelevance that might have seemed to others the salient things about them—say, a load of ornament, once modish, or, in something newer, a pursed air of quaintness or arty simplicism. With the eyes to see past those obstructions, some sensitive soul might have felt, among the Fay's knucklesome chair-legs and davenports, and before the dinted curvilinear sideboard of mahogany, made for some early Victorian, long bankrupt, the emotion of travellers in the Achill Islands, or odd nooks of the Alps, where every-thing in common use, the coracle, the spinning-wheel, the cheese press, seems new and cunning from the hand of the first man making shift on the earth.

Here the three lived, with the heightened, delighted consciousness of an interior that one attains in bed, by firelight, on nights of whining wind and great rain. Each room, behind its window's well-curtained lower half, was a cube of Irish air; the whole house a tiny enclave of Canaan peeled off like a sod and carried down whole, to stand on, in Babylon; when twilight shut England out, Jemmy would sit ravished, with a sense of mental home-coming, to hear the elders plunge off into revels of the headlong, glancing and figured speech that turns and rushes from one splash of vividness on to another still wilder and apter, pouncing here and there on some new detail that catches the eye in this moment's vision and springs a new vision the next, gambolling, fanfaronading, capping itself in drunkennesses of inventive glee, as if the strong cordial of words had been only just crushed by some Noah out of some primal grape.

They had had a week's grand talking now, with Colum at home; what should ail him, he said, not to talk, and he with nothing in all the wide world to be doing but dress a few flies to cast on the waiting snouts of some sizable editors? Articles in divers tones radiated from him by post, Delphic and jaunty, robust and crepuscular, corrective and nourishing; and many came back, for editors were rising badly. "Right off their feed, the creatures. Who'd blame them, and the war upsetting all before it?" Fay said on the night of that day at the club, when he came home and found that one more of his works had returned before him, tumbled, with a pin through it.

His wife read out letters from Ireland—each name, each unit of news like some speck of a printed page for her voice to frame in marginal addenda of biography. Some one was dead, and "Dear, but that wife of his was the torment, and he that was thought such a match for her; very well off he was and high up in the fifties—he'd jilted a couple of ladies before, and would have left her, but they held him to it and when she got married she worried the life out of him; aye, and them all. If a tenant came near her that hadn't holes on his elbows and knees she'd have the rent raised on him." Or a priest would be mentioned, and "That Father Tom was the big-minded man in his way. He'd no sooner be up than he'd go round to every house in the parish and ask had they sent the children to school—Protestants as well as Catholics. And the enlightened views he had! I don't know where he got them. He always would have his own cow, and not be in a house five minutes before he'd go round throwing open the windows." Or, on news of a wedding: "Eighteen bridesmaids! That's heavy on the man, and he poorly off. His father had once been a gentleman trainer in Cavan, a very quiet, respectable man till he drank; he kept no end of horses and eight or nine men and boys to look after them. The County Monaghan was where they came from—an exceedingly good family and united!—you never saw anything like it. His mother sent him on foot into Dundalk, to be apprenticed. 'I won't give you a horse,' said she, 'or you'd only come back on it.' And from that day he never looked back, and he'd nothing to do but keep steady, to leave all his family settled." To Jemmy, the ten-year-old, the life thus seen, or half seen, transfigured by the gusto of his parents' recollection, was more real, more vehemently and intimately conceived, more importunate in its interest, than any could be imaginably lived in Halland or the darkness of outer England. Taking one broken light with another, as he lay, fuses humi, on his back on the carpet, with his ears agape and his small critic nose flicking with perception, he had pieced together a whole set of poignantly live and transparent-motived people, not spoilt by masks of opaque, stuck immobility, like the faces in the streets, but looking all that they were. Father John, who was only of quite a plain family, but introduced a good deal of modern thought into his sermons, and always great at the giving—he beat all, there, but so proud—it was a poor thing to come near him; grandparents, of course, minutely rendered, but also whole casts of minor parts in households raised to movingly high powers of reality; some workman perhaps, in whom angels of light and the pit contended in a vintner grand-father's yard—a great cooper, but you'd need to have your eye on him; he couldn't stand the noise of the wine moving in the casks; or an uncle's cook so asthmatic she'd have a chair there on the landing to sit a while, and she going upstairs; or the friend that " had tremendous taste in china but the drawing-room too crowded with this and that, and the waste! The extravagance! Company morning till night and a set of sables you'd think, if you blew into it, it was quite white; in giving you tea she'd fill the saucer as much as the cup." Places, too; Drogheda—"Ah, that was the real ecclesiastical town—all banks and convents and churches," and summer Mornington, where "the houses you'd lodge in were owned by captains of sailing-ships"—round the walls there'd be pictures of all the story of Joseph, they'd brought back from England; figured thus, as a curious import to a place where everything mattered, even an everyday English thing rose above dusty commonness. Into talk of these people and things the Fays would let themselves in, all three, when they pleased, as by turning a handle you pass from the blown dust of roads to a lawn by the Thames. It was an inlet to intoxicating glows and stirs of thought for Jemmy, supine in a troubled ecstasy with a Freeman's Journal over his face to spare the bashfulness of his happiness in taking his own part in bouts of imaginary repartee and heady duels of brilliant effrontery. For the moment, to-night, the spirit was slightly congealed; it is apt to be that, when an income expires, leaving no visible heir. From thoughts on the dearness of life by the waters of Babylon, Mrs. Fay found only a tragic semi-relief in descants on the milk and honey with which Canaan had flowed. A checking, invincible candour would break off to own that good, of a kind, could come out of Halland. The bacon she would not impeach—"Of course it hadn't the flavour of Irish bacon, but still—" Tea, too, was value for the money—"You wouldn't get better in Dublin." Such things shone with the forced brilliancy of rare good deeds in a naughty world of grasping painters, fishmongers, fruiterers, pike and cormorants of all kinds, fallen far from grace as grace had abounded in Cavan. "Think of that great house"—her father's—"in Grattan Street—it done in first-rate style, top to bottom, four coats of oil paint, every banister bronzed, for sixteen pounds. And such salmon, fresh out of the river—the men would bring it up straight from the beach to the house—fourpence and five-pence a pound; and beautiful fowls, a shilling and one and sixpence; eggs, sixpence a dozen, new laid; and the splendid cauliflowers brought round to the door—ten for sixpence."

In a brooding pause a bell rang in the basement, the old kind of bell that hung sensitively from the end of a springy coil of metal band and tinkled off into silence lingeringly as taps cease dripping. Jemmy rose at once, as one about an appointed business, stood on a chair to peer cautiously out of the window, through the early twilight, to the Grecian porch, pronounced it "Postman" and, descending, took a bunch of keys that hung from one of its number, a redoubtable skewer-like piece, buried to its handle in the rich red timber wall of the sideboard, the stout ark of the Victorian bankrupt's transient glory, and sedately left the room.

His mother considered his retreating figure. "That boy," she said, "will want a suit before the spring."

"Faith, I hope he'll find one in the letter-box," said Fay.

"A cheque, is it, you mean?"

"Aye do I, from the Anglo-Saxon Monthly."

"For the Naval Boilers article, or what?"

"That, and th' one on 'Tendrils of Empire'—or word, maybe, from this review that they have starting, th' Imperial Thinker, that they'll take that other stuff."

"Th' 'Want of Seriousness at the War Office,' is it?"

"Aye. That'd be the haul. Five articles. But there's one I'd liefer see taken than any."

"What's that, then?"

"Just the one on the fishing we had down in Galway the year we were married."

"Oh?" She did not quite see. That good time, remembered, was hers and his. Why let any strange people into their garden?

"I've the wish in my mind, for a while back, it wasn't the way it is with the writing. It's no thing at all to be doin', to keep spillin' over with blather, the way of a wheel-barrow half full of water, and it just as apt to go this way as that, and all about nothing that ever was in the world, for any signs I see. I'd be shut of it all, from this out, but the sorrow's in the set I write for—they can't endure it if you know what you're about. If you do, you're just kept down to sayin' it, bare and plainly, you're that wild for gettin' it out; it's like callin' for help, and the creatures can't bear it—it seems all naked and chilly to them, they're that used to have all they read fluffsome and woolly. Th' ind of it is they've a notion you don't know, really. See th' indless content of Brumby, beyond, and Pinn, when I've mixed 'em the full of the trough, and it not worth the dust you'd see blowin' along the road. An' there's that Galway article back on us twice, and I question will annyone print it, and I that have only to shut my eyes and I'd draw—if I knew how to draw—the curl of the eddy on every snag in the reaches below by Dromore."

"Yes, dear knows," she said. Both had their eyes shut.

"Aye, and the sand on hot days, weeny rafts of it, floatin' off dry on the rise of the tide." He opened his eyes on the gravely-re-entering Temmy. "Well, what was in it?"

Jemmy, with a wrinkled front, was sifting the presumptive values of the take. "Three advertisements— no, two advertisements, three real letters, an' some long strip of a thing from the—Country House, is it?"

"Quick, child—why, what are you about?" To the Country House, the great out-of-doors paper, the essay in veracity had last gone on offer. Fay interrogated the envelope with procrastinating fingers, eager to guess, afraid to know. "If it's a proof! Too fat, I'll engage; not a rustle in it." Hope had already gone when he took out a typed paper, too well known, and a letter, from which he read out, impressionistically, disengaging the essential touches: "'Editor—regrets—subject attractive, but—to interest general reader—long first-hand acquaintance with country described—almost indispensable.' That's the way of it."

She came over and stood behind him, putting a speaking and sustaining palm under each of his cheeks.

"Don't mind them, Colum, anny of them," and then, stroking the hair back from the face, "Colum!"

"Dearie?"

"There's grand wear left in the suit that Jemmy has on, now I look at the front of him."

"Ah, then, is there?" he said, understanding for a minute they said, through her hand and his hair, things that words might have bungled in telling. At the minute's end he opened one of the "real" letters. "Here's the fine suit for the child," he said—it seemed with unflecked pleasure—' and boots, and dear knows what. Th' Imperial Thinker 'll have the pack of them." "Army Reform were they on?"

"Aye, five bulgin' articles, every wan the weight ov lead. You couldn't read them. Wasn't I the wise man to keep out of wars and armies all my life? If I'd as much as seen a troopship fill at Queenstown I'll engage they'd not have had me for a military expert now."

"You're a gifted man," she said, not with the whole mind; unformed thoughts were rising.

Jemmy, too, had his thoughts. "A mil'tary expert?" he asked. "Then sure you'll be able to help stop the frightful recruiting in Ireland. Five hundred enlisted last month, it says in the Freeman beyond, and it treason to Ireland."

"'Deed is it," his mother assented, her whole mind now in the words.

"Aye," Fay admitted, uneasy, not facing her, pleading rather to Jemmy. " That, or, it may be, half the pitaties gone, and it not Christmas; and then there'll be two lads, or three, in the place, and one of them has the thought in his mind, if he quits, the pitaties that's in it will last out the twelvemonth." The imaginative plea grew real to him as he worked on it. "I'll engage that's the way of it, often," he said with conviction, and faced her eye.

She was softened, not turned. "I don't say it's easy," she said, "to be doin' what's right."

He opened another letter, and gave a sharp "Ah!"

"What's that you have there?" she asked, wrenching off from her thoughts.

"Work, I'll be bound—an offer. Did I tell you about the man Roads they have at the club?"

"Roads. That's not an Irish name."

"Moses P. Roads. It is not. He's here startin' a paper, and nothin' will do him but tramplin' the life out of Brumby and Pinn. He'll call, he says, early this evening. That's anny time now."

"Jemmy, tidy those things out of that," said Mrs. Fay first, with a quicker, guiltier, feminine sense of the unspecialized use of an interior. They did all but sleep in the dining-room. "Is it leaders he'll want, like the others?" she then said to Fay.

The bell rang again, remote in the vacuous basement. "We'll be apt to know soon," Fay replied, "and he there mountin' the stairs." Satanic calm, as if he smelt mischief, was settling on him. He opened another letter. But no steps came, only a second ring, the crashing toe of its first note kicking the last dragging heel of the earlier peal.

"Is the girl not below?" Fay asked.

"She is not. I forgot. I let her go off to the Bible-class that she has and not be burning the gas in the kitchen—it's no use only blackening the ceiling."

"Jemmy," said Fay, "will you go to the door? Don't hurry. It's no harm, but good, he'll get from the waiting. Molly," he went on again, with the last-opened letter in one hand, when Jemmy was gone, "you remember the boy in a scrape at the Warder?"

"I do. How at all does he get on, I wonder?"

Fay looked at the letter. "He tells me. He's just been put out of it."

"Dismissed?"

"Aye, is he."

"I thought he was the man's own nephew?"

"Nephew an' all, he's put out of it. Brumby, you see, has the full of his head of pet phrases to feed before spendin' on nephews; and now it's some darlin' rubbish he has about 'men that fail twice failin' always.' 'Knowing men' is what he'd call it—and repeatin' this blather and acting on it'll be ' force of character '; the boy'll be destroyed lest the blather turn out to be nothin' but blather at all."

"Colum, I'll engage there's something we could do."

"We could—" He paused a moment; they heard a fleet foot outside on the landing; far off a heavier one made the lowest stairs creak. "We could put money in our purse," Fay said; he left her to meditate this while he should be handling Roads.

Jemmy entered breathless, fleeing before the caller. "There's a man," he gasped, "coming up. I said he might."

" You did well," said Fay. "'All strange callers are sent by the gods'—you'll find that in Homer. Burrow, small rabbit."

There was, towards a corner, a table; a table-cover, too large for it, hung down to the floor. Jemmy dived under this screen with quiet, purposeful swiftness, as old refugees take cover, or dogs slip under the sofa when bed-time threatens their tenure of the hearthrug. Mrs. Fay took up her sewing, a guard to observant silence; she sat back a little. Fay surveyed the disposition of the forces, found it very good, and, going to the door, let in, not Roads but Brumby.

CHAPTER XIV

I have heard enough since I came here to satisfy me that a cavalier of honour is free to take any part in this civil embroilment whilk he may find most convenient for his own peculiar.
SCOTT, Legend of Montrose, Chap. III

Brumby's way, as he flung Fay a hearty "good evening," was bluff, almost blusterous—a rugged, marrowy Briton greeting his friend, you would say, did you not know as much as you do; knowing it, you would say, what a fine, frank knightly recognition of the dues of courtesy to a foe at his own hearth; and to a foe's wife too; " Good evening, Mrs. Fay," he repeated, sighting her; a whole doctrine of woman's right place in the world was implied in the size and quality of his voice's abatement from its equinoctial breeziness. She froze at the feel of the doctrine; the frost stiffened her bow; then she sat back a little, again, her personality drawn in about her like skirts where mud is, or an army's outposts, the tips of its snailish horns, falling in on it at touch of an enemy unreconnoitred.

Fay, too, had been ineffusive. Worse, he had taken up ground on the hearthrug; there he looked static; and Brumby, born a planet, and aware of it, felt himself adrift in space acted upon more than acting, drawn towards the one infernal heavenly body on the rug and repelled from the other in the chair, the whole disarrangement of forces giving him a perturbed, hovering, dependent motion, not to be put up with. "Might I speak with you one moment?" he said, and waited for the action of the powers that preserve the stars from wrong. None acted. Mrs. Fay did not move. Fay did not offer another room. "Shall I not be boring Mrs. Fay?" he asked. Would nothing lift the world back on to its hinges?

 Nothing. My wife and I are—are friends," Fay said with a nasty dryness.

"That's right, that's right," said brusque geniality. "Insolent beast!" he thought, really; was it for Fays and the like to give people answers to pick out of wrappings of pregnant irrelevance?—"That's right," he repeated and, under the cover of this fusillade, he tried to edge on to the hearthrug.

Fay, too, knew his tactics. "Won't you sit down?" he said suavely.

Brumby sat. There are times when all chairs are dentists'; this time was one; only from that rug could all that he had to say come impromptu; thence he would shine like a sun restored by divine goodness to men, who for their deserts, had walked a good while in darkness. The chair spoilt everything; there was Fay, in the place of the sun, emitting malign or ambiguous moonshine; here was he, the authentic Phoebus Apollo, vouchsafing his light as it were from a hole; when he broke into feeling speech, it rang like some recitation. However, he broke. "My dear fellow, I've come here to do—well, what many would call a hard thing."

Clocks cannot strike twelve whenever they like. Could Brumby have had but five minutes alone, to walk about, buttoning his coat and unbuttoning again, filling his chest, draining at ease the whole bright wine-cup of nobility in conscious action, and then rushed in on Fay and begun, his voice would have plumped clean down on the right note of generous self-prostration, the note possible only to the strong who are so very strong that they can give huge discounts now and again without really and gravely cheapening themselves. As it was, all was blurred; the attack had no precision; wavering between tones, the voice could hold none, till the round, mellow strength it had tried for almost thinned to a whine.

"I'm sorry," said Fay, helpless at hearing the whine.

"Sorry I've come?" Brumby gasped. Was he late then, already?

"No, no; sorry it's hard, of course." Fay almost snapped, cross with himself for softening. But the softness had served; it smote like a Moses' rod upon Brumby, drawing from the Fundamental Gneiss of his nature the waters of generous passion. Brumby leapt from his chair; he found, lifted, shook, swung, and squeezed a hand which Fay vainly charged with the protest of a limp slackness. "Thank you, thank you warmly, my dear chap. I knew you were decent, really; I never thought anything else." Seriously, a little heat of relief from terror really glowed in Brumby. Fay was not gone, past trying for; and then a swift instinct snatched at that heat, to use it; it was a match, a taper; more could be lit from it—perhaps the whole set, unkindled fire of cordiality that had just failed to bum, as it should, in that place; yes, it caught better now, Brumby felt, as he heard his voice roll round the room. "D'you know that all these—forgive me, Mrs. Fay—all these confounded days of misunderstanding and—unpleasantness—all these days that thought has been simply a gastric juice, you know, to me, I do assure you, a gastric juice welling and surging up in me, helping me digest my indignation. I think you'll own I've—had some food for indignation, eh?" The whine was near; rush and assurance were lost again to the voice as it asked for a hand through the dirt.

"Well, personally—" Fay began.

Hand or not. Brumby grabbed it as one. "Thank you," he broke in, before it should pass from him, "for that," and, when Fay tried to speak, "Not a word, now; not a word," he broke in again, clinging to the unspokenness of Fay's next words as if to a life-belt: "Who am I, I should like to know, to ask for more than simply that manly, frank acknowledgment of yours?"

"Acknowledgment?"

"Tut, man! I knew from the first you'd meet frankness half-way, and—" Both paused for a moment; Brumby, for help, but not a rope's end was thrown; Fay, in despair of a hearing.

Then Fay cleared his throat to begin, and Brumby again took fright at the words that might come, and rushed on: "Knowing that, I'll tell you just what I've done." All this being cried out for that place on the hearthrug; where else could he fitly be so noble as he meant to be? Bitten with cruel cravings, he hovered round Fay; his body hankered, like a dog's visibly. Fay winced, but held on; Brumby must just be noble as best he might. "I have simply put behind me everything, everything that"—he cautiously peered at Fay's face and picked each word, with a fumble, to fit what he saw there—"that I—that we—might rather—forget—might some time hereafter be glad to forget, in your—your past treatment of—shall I say, in our previous relations, for, no doubt there were faults—well, mistakes—on both sides—all, you know, miserable sinners—only, it's simply this, that just for my own satisfaction, I'd rather you knew there's no bad blood, whatever, as far as I go, about the—the kind of reticence you know, that you practised upon me, and all that—the use, for instance—in a sense, the very generous use—you made of that stupid boy's copy—he won't cross your path again, be easy about that."

The last words had more ease; here at least, the tone said, with just pride, was a gage of goodwill for you, something solid. Mrs. Fay breathed an "Ah!" and stopped sewing. Fay watched.

Brumby stared. Were they not touched? He went on, his voice grown somewhat lonely: "That dance you led Pinn—you shouldn't have done it, you know, my dear boy—a joke's a joke, I know, and I don't say the first was a bad one to play him—but this last, this getting the poor foolish oaf to go back on his word and—cancel that promise of ours—well, no matter how glad I may be for myself, it was rough on the man, I'm bound to say frankly. But, as far as regards myself, whatever you've done that you'd now wish undone"—from Fay, who was gently shaking his head, Brumby looked, for escape, to the lady, to meet a gaze of distaste and wonder; her eyes had been fixed in this since he spoke of abolishing Dick—"I simply obliterate, I wipe it off my memory." Where a grateful murmur should have prolonged the full stop, he was left to enforce punctuation himself with a wide gesture of rejection. "I put aside every grain of personal feeling. All I remember now is the sterling worth of your work for the Constitutional party."

"Oh, the party?"

The "Oh!" was all but an "Ugh." Brumby himself could not miss the whole force of it. "You're right," he amended in haste, "not merely the party; the nation; it's the spirit of all that's best in our English politics—that's what you've served, not the party alone. England hath need of you."

"England!" Dissimulation was dropping from Fay, whole cloaks at a time.

"Right, again! By Jove, you're right always. What's England? As you say, it's the Empire—that's all that matters. It's the spirit, the august temper of a great governing race—born governing race—that's what we want, and you've got it, if ever man had, and it's our duty, yours and mine, not to stand, for our own feelings' sake, between the Empire and its good. Will you come back? There; thank God, I've had the manliness to see it. Come back, man."

"To the old work?" Fay asked, to gain time. He knew, but he wanted to ask a question of his wife's eyes; but these were down again on the sewing now, where they stayed, though the question reached them through drooped lids. "The old terms?" Fay asked Brumby.

"I should prefer, if I may to offer you another £50 a year. Come, now, you mustn't refuse. The work's hard enough."

"The 'gains of a prostitute pen'—was it you dropped that pearl, the last night we met? Or Pinn? Or was it a chorus? Now, mind, if I come—"

"Yes?"

"It will not be to hear things like that."

"You'll write for us only, you mean? You'll have your whole heart in the paper?"

"Is that a condition you're making?"

"Bless you, no! What should I want with conditions—in view of your break with the Stalwart?"

"No—simply in view of a need that I have to be civilly talked to. You promise?"

"Fay, that fine pride of yours is irresistible. Of course I promise, heartily."

"Then—about your nephew—"

"Was I not quite clear just now? You needn't have the least uneasiness."

"You'll overlook, you mean—"

"Yes, all you did, absolutely."

"Yes, yes, but what he did, or didn't—"

"I know, I know; you might well fear annoyance, with Dick what he is, I'm sorry to say. I simply give you my word you'll not see him again. I go straight from here and dismiss him."

"It's not done already?"

It was, but why—Brumby felt—let Dick's blood go to waste when, by simply post-dating its shedding, it came in so well for sealing a treaty? Again Mrs. Fay looked up, to examine the skin of this unknown species of grub. Fay examined it, too, as it stood there before him, distilling its kind of saliva. Once he began, "Mr. Brumby—" quite seriously; then he stopped, as if he had had some thoughts of throwing a lantern's light through a brick wall, but had given them up. " Oh, you mustn't," he sneered, "scarify your own flesh for my comfort. You'll keep that boy." It was almost an order.

"D'you mean you won't mind?"

"No. I'm that odd. You keep him?"

"You wish it?"

"No end to my eccentricity, is there? It's settled then?" Brumby gave a bewildered assent, a Roman uncle who now must go to his nephew and say he is not quite Roman really. "You want me to-night?" Fay broke in on Brumby's thoughts of this palinode.

"Well, if you could—Albry's speaking again. Will you do him?"

"At ten I'll be there."

"Right! Good night, Mrs. Fay. Good-bye, my dear fellow, at present, and " The lust for a set-piece, a joint pose for them all, was strong in him; yet all was not right; the trumpets would not blow full; "—and all I say is, may our joint work, yours and mine, do more than ever to keep the flag of all that's loyal and frank and generous—all that's essentially English—flying in public life, and—"I'll let you out," said Fay, and Brumby gave up; the luffed sails would not belly.

They gone, Jemmy crept out of cover and sat on the open floor; he looked tired, like one oppressed in mind with the strain of comprehending a portent. "The Lord bless us!" he said, and was plunged again in exhausting reflections.

"Jemmy, Jemmy!" said his mother, remonstrant, yet not dissentient.

The bang of the front door brought Jemmy to; he clambered to the window for a sight of the departing monster.

"Colum, what made you give in, and Mr. Roads coming at any time?" Mrs. Fay asked, as Fay entered.

"Did you not see the state he was in, fit to go on his knees on the floor, or dear knows what?"

"Ah, then, and why not let him be rollin' his own little dirty hoop for himself?"

"What! And he apt to sling himself over a bridge, he's that desprit, or take the head off him the time he'd be shaving!"

"Is it he? I question will he. You'd need have a sort of a spunk to do that."

But still the voice of the weaker vessel was merciful.

"Playin' at David, again," he said, " that's what he'd be, an' killing Goliaths an' all before him. You wouldn't destroy his play on him, you cruel woman, and he beggin' an' cryin', or very close on for the bits of smooth stones we have here in the brook, the poor foolish old child? "

"Father," Jemmy reported from the window, "th' abominable man was here just now is talking to another."

Fay peered down into the twilight. "It's Roads," he whispered and then, at a moment's end, "they're off and away, colloguin,' out of the street." He came back pensive from the window. " Will Roads be for not cornin' nigh us, I wonder, from this out?" Then, with a sigh that uncouples a mood, care yielded to business. "Do you think," he asked, " you've the time to get on with that leader?"

"The one for that man?"

"Aye, upon that speech of Albry's—it's not long before he'll be at it."

She unhooded a typing machine, sat down, and looked up at him, ready. He dictated in dull, level tones:

"'With a painful exactitude, passing at times into contemptuous pity. Lord Albry pointed out last night the lack of dignity, the abject touting for votes, the—"

She looked up a moment. " Ah, then, he might not say it to-night," her caution objected.

"He will if he lives," said Fay's larger experience. He went on, dictating:

"'—the curious depths of self-abasement which the machine politicians now dominant at Radical headquarters have forced upon their titular leader, the—'"

A ring came, below. " Roads, after all!" Fay said. The ring was repeated louder. "And the temper gone on him," Fay added.

"Jemmy, there's a good boy," said his mother, and Jemmy went out. She extinguished the machine. Their ears felt for the grind of the unoiled latch and the creak of the hinges of the door down below, and then for the bounding step of Jemmy as he fled aloft before the ascending guest. Was that quite the way, his mother chid him, to treat Mr. Roads?

"Roads! Not at all! It's wan Pinn—or he says so."

Jemmy's last words came, muffled, from under the pendent screen of his earth.

Fay laughed. "Begob, is Goliath here now for his sword and his spear?"

CHAPTER XV

And behold another beast, a second, like to a bear.
DANIEL vii. 5

It was partly that Pinn was not very well-bred, partly that bows and so forth are mere forms and this was no time for forms; anyhow, Pinn did not notice the lady at all—did not indeed, salute even Fay formally; he just came in and put down his hat and then went with all his might at that which his hand had found to do, as a workhouse doctor goes straight at a case without offering any delightful nothings about the weather. Fay looked across to his wife, his eyelids lifted. "You see," they said, "the kind of savage." Rude things done to himself nearly always diverted him; this made him angry, and, so self-possessed. Anger enough will always lay shyness.

"I've not come here," Pinn began, "to—"

"Good evening," Fay interrupted with a corrective blandness, as a composed elder sets aside a child's false start in manners.

Pinn stared, almost jumped. Still, he came back, toed the line and started again. "Good evening," he said—even now it was only to Fay—"I've not come here, I should tell you before I go further, to unsay one word of—"

"No?" said Fay. "Then—"

His eye with a leading expression, travelled towards the door.

"Good God, man," Pinn cried, a note of incipient dismay sounding cracked through the full blare of bullying rectitude, "only last night, when by no wish of mine, you were given a chance to redeem your—your—" He spluttered, seeking a word black to match Fay's roll of iniquities.

"Your?" Fay prompted him suavely, "your—shall we say, your own promise to Brumby?"

"No, sir, your past," stormed the figure of flustered virtue; " only last night, it seems, you must needs pass off as yours the work of another man!"

"And I not an editor, even!" Fay murmured.

The shocked tone was audible clearly. Pinn could not afford, though, to hear. "What," he ground on, ostentatiously set on his own run of thought, " what, in the name of all that's true, am I to think of you; what am I to think of you?" By the second "think," the emphasis had grown prodigious. Sufferer and nurse in one, he rocked himself in a paroxysm of pity for the pain it gave him to put hand again to so dirty a tool.

Fay's knuckles, for once, poked out through the glove. "I can express, as you know, a good many things, but my indifference to what you think of me—" He shrugged. "No, there's no doing it."

The blow, given, half eased and half sickened the striker; mere punching is apt to. To Pinn, the suddenly pummelled, the world reeled and was changed; duty alone changed not; thunderous as ever, she roared to him still the old order to make for that which he wanted. And he would; he was staunch; only, if he must make for it barefooted, like this, across red-hot ploughshares, he would at least go the nearest way. "I think," he said in a hard-held voice, "I had better be plain. If I overlook all that is past—if I take you back to your post, will you give me an absolute promise to do no other work of a similar kind for anyone else?"

"Oh, no! No promise of any sort," Fay murmured, shaking his head quite gently, as if in rejection of some speculative proposition of small moment. "Oh, no! "

Pinn's entire experience as a dealer in literary labour came to the ground in one piece. "No! Then—" He gave one fierce downward jerk to his waistcoat with both hands, swept a sleeve swiftly, with a peremptory air of departure, round a quadrant of his hat, and turned to the door; he even made a step towards it; how instinctive in us all, by this time, is the traditional "business" in the standard drama of insulted worth! And yet in the time of taking that step he had re-taken hold of the horrible truth that here was no drama, as drama should be; all was derailed; not for him the flaming, towering exit of flouted and mud-pelted dignity; the price was prohibitive. Then, once more, Nature, the milky mother, the all-providing, put tactics into his heart that he was not conscious of framing; he turned again quickly to Fay; he softened; he yearned towards him almost, speaking to him in the voice of the mere looker-on, the humane looker-on, who cannot stand by and see a man drift to his ruin. "Moloney," he started.

"Fay." Moloney served to grace my measure, but Fay was still my real name. "You remember the verses?"

If there was a thing Pinn hated, it was a quotation made just in this way from that larger hemisphere of letters which he had not travelled. However, he stomached it, things being desperate.

"Mr. Fay," he began again, the benevolent onlooker's tone very slightly impaired, "you have a wife."

''You see that—at last?''

A sheepish bow, minutely acknowledged by Mrs. Fay, was extorted from Pinn. Then, to Fay, in low, earnest tones of remonstrance: "Have you, before refusing my offer—have you—I'm a husband myself and I ask—thought of her?"

"I have—and of your having failed to, just now. 'There's a form in these things, Mr. Pinn, there's a form.' You remember the passage?"

Whipped to a fury by these flippancies Pinn emitted a "Very well, sir!" of ultra-finality—you would have thought—and made again for the door. That door was impassable. It led, not to an oil-clothed landing and stairs, but to a vertical drop into abolition, the death of his personality, as men had felt it, all its individual, urgent push and pressure. He could not walk across that door-mat into annulment. It headed him back, it drove him on to Fay again, this time with a corrugated forehead, a tone of earnest, perplexed speculation, divorced from all worldly interests, from everything concrete. "Mr. Fay, I can't make you out."

"Need you?"

"Need!" Pinn drew nearer, amazed, confounded, that any man should raise such a question. "Surely I need. Mustn't his world be a whole to each man—ordered, a system? To give up that, to give up the hope of that, the effort at that, would be death in the mind. And of my world, for good or evil, you are a part." Fay gave a grunt. "Aye, and a part of some moment." Fay grunted again; Pinn, to keep going at all, had to take up the grunt as a modest disclaimer. "Surely you cannot but know you have gifts of—I may say, rare gifts. Oh, I don't blind myself to the moral transgression—the Warder entanglement—"

"Need we—?" Again that leading look towards the door. But beyond it were darkness and gnashing of teeth. Pinn tore on, shunning arrest. "Still, I do think—you'll say if I'm wrong—" Fay groaned rather than grunted his disrelish for the post of arbiter—"but I do think I've got at the key to that little—that little lapse on your part—found it, you must let me say, in the inferiority of your Warder work."

"Oh! You're free to judge." Weary of deprecation, Fay let the noise run on.

"Am I free to conjecture, too—that over there at the Warder your own convictions have never found real expression?"

"Dear me, yes. Do conjecture—anything."

"That in fact, the expression by you of Tory prejudice there was nothing but, shall I say, irony?"

"Eh?" said Fay, listening now. That Pinn should so much as conceive the idea of irony piqued him.

"Irony used, shall I say, in the spirit of drama, just as Shakespeare, no doubt, had to keep down his own progressive convictions in order to write, as you'll notice, the most Tory speeches he gives to one of his characters, Coriolanus?"

"And others for Cade, the least bit different, eh?"

"Precisely. Speeches for reactionaries of all shades," assented Pinn; his Tudor studies had limits. "So, as I take it, your Warder leaders were just dramatic efforts, written in imaginative sympathy—and that, too, tinged with sarcasm, and the views were not yours at all."

"You know, that's not ill put," said Fay, as if to a boy whose cerebral night had admitted a first ray.

"You think so?" Pinn cried hungrily. A drowning man would grab at a scythe, to be saved; give him a barbed wire life-line, he'll tie it on, naked. Pinn flung himself on to Fay's words of indulgent contempt; he twisted them into the longed-for assent. "In that case," he said, before Fay could say more, "I am bound, as a clear-headed man, to withdraw, unreservedly, any reflections I made last week on your conduct."

Fay, with his feeble pity for all souls in trouble, winced to see this one, the second that night, sneaking, at its own different gait, down the same via dolorosa. "Unreservedly?" he asked; the voice tried to ride trim, but the list to the side of compunction was monstrous.

"Absolutely! Unreservedly! Thank God, I know how to face facts and say, on cause shown—'I was wrong.'"

"Thank you, thank you," Fay muttered evasively; his eyes shirked the sweat on Pinn's soiled-parchment face; like distilled water turbid, the drops, as they ran and paused, and ran again, looked so foul and yet so insipid.

"And now," Pinn went on, "let me offer a practical proof of good faith. Will you take up your work again as leader-writer to the Stalwart? "

"At the—old hours?" Fay asked, to say something.

Then, Pinn, trembling, took heart a little. Fay back at all would be much; Fay back with a warrant against traffic with the Midianites—how much more would that be!—"Might I suggest an hour earlier at both ends—to come and to go—that is, if you don't mind?"

"I do," Fay said, and the silence of the next seconds, in which he did not give a reason for minding, defined their future relations.

"Oh, I don't press it." Thus did Pinn sign the definition; and then some god with a humour as grisly as an imp's on Notre Dame put it in the glum man's head to try the uses of playfulness. "Only, remember!" he said, "no irony! No drama!" The red of his first shame had sunk, but the sweat was wet still; where the wrenched laugh crumpled his face the blobs ran together, like drops of rain on a pane, and made greyish puddles in vales of dull grey.

"Remember," said Fay pretty grimly, "'absolutely, unreservedly.'"

"True!" That game was up. The wrinkled paste of the grin that had not been of use was rolled out, and the sweat held up in its folds was undammed and flowed ticklingly in among the sparse wires of Pinn's beard. He scratched the teased chin. "You'd be ready—to-night? " His voice was quite timid.

"Yes. One o'clock, then, as usual?"

"Albry, second speech—eh? For the leader? Right well you wrote on his first. Will you?"

"Yes." Fay had not known till now how easy, when done in its place, the regal monosyllable is—the one-word speech that the tongue can bestow like a cut gem, from the moment when others must take it so. Then, too, for the first time, he found he could give the look that tells somebody else he may go. Pinn bowed good night to the lady, punctiliously now; he was well broken in; Fay made a slight feint to escort him downstairs. " Don't stir," said Pinn; he embraced like a very boon the insult of the unmeant civility I'll let myself out."

"Can you? At one, then." Fay nodded; he had learnt to nod, too, and Pinn got out as he could; he did not exactly walk backwards, but Jemmy's eye, stuck to a place where the table-cover had worn to a net, could see, all the way, an edge of the grey face.

Then Jemmy crept out again, silent and prostrate at first, as before, with giving to new and dreadful images admittance into the soul. "Aren't they the desperate set, the two of them?" he said, when again himself, to his silent parents.

"'Deed are they!" said his mother, with conviction. "You'll be off to bed, dear, now," she added presently.

Jemmy's good nights filled part of a difficult pause. Then the two elders were left, the listening mind of the one enduring the upbraiding of the other, both silent.

"Ach, an' he in the state that he was—doing every Station of the Cross before our eyes!" Fay broke out once, that one shred, of all the silent dialogue, emerging into audibility; so the tip of one peak, out of whole ranges of coral, will rise clear of the sea.

The dialogue broke off. "You'd like to go on?" she said; she went to the typewriter. The interrupted leader lay there.

"Not that one. I'll do that at Brumby's the best way I can. Pinn's I'd liefer see over and done with the way it would not be the weight of the world on my mind, lest I go off to sleep in a chair and I writing on till dear knows when in the morning. Shall we make just an offer to get it done?"

She took out the half-typed page and put in a clean one. He dictated; his voice was just as before:

"'The methods by which Lord Albry, during the past four years, has lowered so gravely the standard of responsibility in English public life received painful illustration in his speech of last night. The groundless detraction, the—'"

"Colum!" she broke out, and then stuck.

"Dear one?"

"Colum, I don't like at all what you're doing."

"Eh?" he said guiltily.

"Partly, your health. It's the work of two days every evening."

"Ah, then, whisht gabbin', dear child," he laughed, much relieved. "Say, no work at all, and that's what it is, but whistlin' old tunes, and that only. Attend now." He spouted again, and the outflow, facile before, was now quite ostentatiously effortless:

"'The groundless detraction, the frivolous swash-buckling, the violence tempered only by levity, were all exemplified. The—'"

"Colum," she burst in again, " it's not the health only. It's this—is it right of us?"

"Ah!" said Fay. So the trouble was come. All across the sky he had seen the cloud marching upon him; here was the first drop splashed from it. And then, for one moment, it held off; or, at least, he could shelter. For now, when rings at the door no longer came laden with moment, one tinkled below and tailed off into silence. "I'll go," said Fay, jumping up. Jemmy gone, there was no one to answer it. Alone, she walked up and down, suddenly stopping, then going on, pricked, past sitting still, by the thing she had not said. Her lips, when the door re-opened, were framing to say it, but through the door came, not Fay only, bearing some letter, but Fay introducing, now when the thought of him was past, the much-postponed Roads.

CHAPTER XVI

So sinks the day-star in the ocean bed,
And yet anon repairs his drooping head,
And tricks his beams, and with new-spangled ore
Flames in the forehead of the morning sky.
MILTON, Lycidas

Roads was more at his ease than any mere note of his doings can tell; each joint of his jaws and limbs worked greasily with a lubricant self-satisfaction; words swished unctuously out of him; the facile insolence ran sweet on its cool ball bearings. "A true wife, I see!" He leered engagingly at the two chairs by the writing-table. "Well"—he plumped into the softest of the others—"I've known fools call me a cynic, but those two chairs do me good." The act of seating his body flowed rhythmically into that of finding his cigars. And as with his action, so with his voice. A break there certainly was between one group of words and the next, but a purr of continuous sound ran on, as a working gramophone murmurs across the blanks between bursts of articulate noise. Each speech was the second stage of Creation—not a making of something where nothing had been; rather, what had been void took form. "And now"—the spirit of Roads moved again on the face of the waters—"if Mrs. Fay will allow two Bohemians—you'll join me?"

"Thanks. No."

"Not? And you think you're a journalist? Well"—Roads picked a cigar for himself—"if Mrs. Fay will allow one Bohemian—"

"My wife is not leaving us," Fay said, and eyed the cigar, as Roads felt, rudely. From boyhood, you see, Roads, when going by train, had always jumped into non-smoking compartments, as being less crowded and stuffy, and had then filled his pipe, lit a match, and courteously said, with his thumb jamming down the tobacco, "Objection to smoking?"; so he felt, very fairly, that courtesy should be returned. In a working journalist, too, meeting a man of position, the want of politeness was complicated with a want of sense, which distressed a clear mind. But Roads was not there to give away knowledge of life; he was a business man on a business errand. So he only purred a little less as he put his cigar-case away and made him a second opening out of the way his first had been countered.

"I like you," he said; " you're straight. And you're able to write. You know that?"

"In the sense you mean—yes."

"And you—now, I'll be straight too—you want money? "

"I find it has uses. And you?"

"I've the money, and I want your stuff. It's good. See, I don't beat you down. It's good."

"It? What, exactly—?"

"What do I go by? Well"—he hung a moment savouring his own shrewdness—"which would you rather I went by? Stalwart—eh? Or Warder?" He twinkled with happy, contained roguishness. Fay, with a gesture, disclaimed desire to guide the selection of samples. "You see, I know a thing or two—two things in fact—" the shrewd man babbled on.

"I see."

"You mean, how do I know? Well, not by asking. You don't want to ask. I just stood still, and let 'em ram it into me."

"Them? Yes, I see."

"Finn first; two hours ago; he came round to me—'Simply a matter of duty,' you know, and all that—must ' put me on my guard '; see?"

"Against me? Yes."

"He'd given you a chance, he said; found you didn't know the work; up to tricks, too. 'I had to fire him out,' he said—no, 'terminated his engagement'—that was it—'a fortnight ago.'"

Fay fingered Roads' note, with expression. Pinn's testimonial, alone, would scarcely explain it.

Roads met the interrogation. "You see he'd a slave-of-conscience look on him that thick, a fool could tell he was up to some game. So I breathed my gratitude—just a few broken words, y' know; I'd needed telling that I said—hadn't known you wrote at all. He coughed a bit. 'You'd like,' he said, 'to see some of his stuff, and judge for yourself? ' he says, anxious-like. 'Well,' I said. 'Well? ' I always let 'em run their own heads into it. 'Seen the Warder's leaders all last week?' he says. 'No,' I said, 'thank God,' just to be nice to him. 'Well,' he says, 'if you want to know Fay's hand, I'm told he has had work at the Warder. Verb sap,' he says, and then he 'oofed out of it. Well, I didn't read the Warder. I got thinking. Last Tuesday week, he said, he'd fired you. Very next day the Stalwart had the leader that knocked 'em at the club. Was it you wrote it?—I thought I'd just come round and ask; so I wrote."

"Well—" Fay was beginning.

Roads, radiant, stopped him. "Oh, no need, now. What don't I know, now? Why, I met the other beauty on your doorstep. He jumped first; then he looked sad. 'Don't mind me,' he says, 'I'm a little upset, for I've just done the beastliest job of my life. I've just sacked a man in that house,' he says, ' and I know he's a rotten bad man at his trade, and a nasty untrustworthy fellow, but then there's a wife,' he says, 'there's a child; I can't forget that,' he says. I walked him a bit up the street. 'One does feel it,' I said, ' though the beggar, maybe, has only been with you some days.' 'It's years,' he snivelled—'this one.' My turn to jump, hearin' that. I knew some game had been on, and here was Pinn's game getting queered with this other old hen starting in playing across the one pitch. Between 'em they pretty well indexed the whole of your stuff before I let go—leaders, music, the whole boiling. Now—d'you know?—it's good."

Fay bowed. Roads amplified the tribute. "Rot, you know, really—I know that as well as yourself—but rot that tells; it goes home to folk—shows 'em they're really doing a duty where anyone might have thought they were only just getting a knife into folk they'd a down on. Then, the way you hand out the good marks to those fiddlers—well, I can't read that sort of thing myself—never could, except once in a way, when I have to, for business—but even then it almost makes a plain business man feel he could show whole orchestras the way to do it. It's upliftin' to the public." Fay again bowed, with due gravity. "But, I say," Roads went on, "ain't you tired—even if you hadn't lost these jobs of yours—ain't you tired of playing up to only half your public—pretty short half, too—two out of ten more like. D'you never think of writing at the whole lot—right at the whole country?"

"The country?"

"What's the country, you're asking? I'll tell you. D'y'ever observe—" But here Roads in his turn was invaded by the monologist's craving for the hearthrug. "Would you not make him sit in a chair, this poor, tired husband of yours?" he asked.

"Perhaps Mr. Roads would be happier," Mrs. Fay said. A stress on the " happier" warned Fay against feckless softenings presently. Fay sat.

"D'y'ever notice," Roads resumed, rising, it seemed, in abstraction, and taking the tribune, "that, of every ten men you know, there's two shall we say, that wouldn't vote Radical—not if an angel came down with a shout, just to make 'em? Now, are those two the country?"

"I don't say that."

"Brumby, the bat, does. They're not, though. I'm a Conservative myself, in private life, and yet I say they're not. That's two. There's other two wouldn't vote Tory for all the angels in the Primrose League. Are they the country, then?"

"Oh, I don't say that either."

"Pinn does, the old moth! And they ain't, as you say, either. Why, those four make just nought, the one brace equalling and destroying th' other brace, plus and minus, same as algebra, and more than half the country—six in ten—not hove in sight yet. Six in ten? Eight in ten, more like. And where are they, all this time? Sitting at home; minding their little bit of betting; taking a sup of beer—to it a draw of 'baccy; formin' instructed views on Saturday's League matches; except there's talk, shall we say, of puttin' up a war, and then, with th' instincts of perfect sportsmen, they're up and out of the house in an instant of time, hollerin' out, 'Go Nap,' on a soft thing, or ' God's sake, pass—it's a wrong 'un.' Rest of the time the other four men, Pinn's lot and Brumby's lot, think out the issues and that, and vote same way as last time, just holdin' each other, and so nothing happens, till one of the sterling six, the Old Guard, no frothin' politicians, but the bone and sinew of the nation, comes up and says: ' I don't rightly know about such things,' he'll say, ' thank God! and don't care; but here goes, anyway,' he'll say, and he'll sling his vote—p'r'aps for a man that keeps a good horse, p'r'aps for a man that looks evenly fed on a platform— and Cab'nets rise and perish. It's constitutional government. Now, I know those six men. You think I'm vain, to say it?"

"No, no."

"I say it, anyhow, and chance it. Know 'em? Why, how shouldn't I, and every bar alive with 'em! And what I say is this—isn't the Press to stand by those men? Shan't it read the souls of those six—eight, still, strong men? Ain't some piercin', glowin' mind, same as yours, to fix and stiffen up for 'em their every impulse, givin' it just the backin' of sound principle they hadn't 'ad the time to think of—how should they, with the lot o' things they have to see to? Sir, it's—it's the strongest game that's waiting to be played in journalism. Understan' me?"

"You're limpid."

"The strongest game in journalism. And I can't play it. See, I'm straight—I tell you 'ow it's got to be played, but I can't do it—not alone; for I can't write, never could. You can. One thing, you've got the knack of slanging folk in a broad, judicial spirit, not roarin' and stamping like Brumby and Pinn, as if you could see there was no one listenin', but lickin' your tongue quiet and oily and gentle round the curse words till it's like a whole court was holdin' its breath while the beak starts to dress down a coster that hasn't remembered his manners."

Fay bowed again, and the stream ran on: "Here's another point—if you've written well, as I said, how much better you'll write, with all the scope you'll have—voicin' every mood, of the country; one day it's weariness like when it's a bit off it—not having any serious politics to-day, thanks—only a feelin' of the hollowness of things; and then, come next week, its buoyant optimism an' firm, crisp 'old on life, and what not! All that range and freedom after the crampy lines you've had to work on, damnin' one small lot of cranks to buck up another. Why, you've only to give your own powers free play at giving the country the thing that the country wants—the six-man country, mind you—no potty two-man country for us!—and there'll be an itch a day in six heads out o' ten till they've read your stuff. Itch!—it's there now, waiting for us two to rub it—you, in my paper. I put it straight now—will you?"

"There's one thing," Fay said suspensively. "Yes?" Roads craned to hear.

"It's merely a point of—oh, I suppose the thing to say's—conscience."

Roads grew anxious. "One moment," he said, "I love a conscientious mane—"

"The affection shines through you," Fay said very softly. '"—by which I mean a man of strong conscience, healthy conscience, not of a conscience that can't go out when it rains."

"Yes, yes, we're all fine, robust moralists; but I'm not being noble just now. I'm serious. My point is
"

"Do let it be serious, indeed, if it's for it you won't take a lift out of the old party ditch."

"That!" Fay grimaced. "No. It's a point of what you might call honesty."

"Don't be a faddist, now." Fear again overcast Roads.

"Honesty—towards you."

"Well, if that's all?"

"It's this. I don't want to give to your work the hours at which most leaders are written." Roads was hilarious. "Bless you, I don't want those. Why, we'll be all through the North by the time the old stick-in-the-muds start the night's work. Good Lord, if they hadn't sacked you, you'd have time to do our little job and then go round and put each of them in a bit for himself." Roads roared at his fantasy.

"In that case—" Fay looked at his wife; then not being helped, he decided alone.

"You'll stand in?" Roads said cheerily.

"Yes, provided, of course—"

"Ah, I think we'll meet as to terms." The economic value of high wages was one of the secrets Roads had mastered; the mastery steeled him to give them with unaffected freedom from pain. "Shall we—now? Or later?"

"Later—d'you mind?" Fay looked at the clock. He had learnt fluency in rudeness to-night.

"Sacked you, did they?" Roads chuckled to Fay as Fay let him into the street. "We'll teach 'em."

Fay came up the stairs, not at ease. He had cause. "Colum," his wife said, checking her pacing round the carpet, "I'm not happy."

He held her still, imprisoning and caressing. "Love, love, what is it?"

"They had me tormented enough already, the two that were in it before."

"Fearing for your Susannah, eh?" His voice played and consoled, like a stroking hand. "And now there are three elders?"

She was past stroking. "That's the way, Colum—you joke, and I wretched."

"Ah, then, what is it, my darling? You 'don't think it right,' was it? Cruel, is what what you mean, of me—pickin' up all these grubs and worms, the way that you'd see an old bird, an' stuffin' them into the bill of the Jemmy that's now busy roostin' above there?"

"Ach, I don't mind them at all!" She spurned the idea. "It's—"

"What, dear one?"

"Colum, you have a great turn for the writing. Don't use it to do wrong."

"Is it"—comprehension dawned—"harm Ireland?"

"Aye is it—help them that harm her. Not in your right mind—I know; you're a good man, Colum; you wouldn't; but then don't I know the way that it is with the writing—the way lights come out, and you going on, and things run in clear on you. It is then, before you knew it at all, you might some time or other be seeing—the way it'd be, written up on a wall—the thing'd be good for England to do for herself an' not Ireland."

"And saying it?"

"Before you knew, perhaps, at all."

"Ah, then, I'm not that bad." He was tenderly remonstrant; the kiss, like a pledge, soothed her. "Shall we on?" he said, and she went to the typewriter. "The one for the Stalwart?" he asked, and began, at her nod, to dictate:

"'Is there, we venture to ask, no limit to the permissible economy of truth?'"

"Have you that?" he asked in a moment.

She clicked in two last letters. "Yes."

The work proceeded. Displaced things, which had had to move roughly back into place, moved smoothly on in their places again.

Charles Edward Montague was born in London on New Year's Day, 1867.

Montague was the son of Francis Montague, an Irish Roman Catholic priest from County Tyrone, Ireland, who after falling in love with Rosa McCabe, the daughter of a successful merchant from Drogheda, left the Church, married Rosa and, in 1863, moved to England.

His education was excellent; he attended the City of London School and then went on to university at Balliol College, Oxford.

Whilst at Oxford he achieved, in 1887, a First in Classical Moderations and two years later a Second in Literae Humaniores.

In addition to his time studying Montague, a keen writer, wrote several and well-respected literary reviews for the Manchester Guardian.

In February, 1890, the editor, C. P. Scott, invited him to Manchester for a month's trial at the paper. Montague was obviously an impressive young man and he was soon given a full-time job.

It was here that Montague was to begin his career in earnest; his hard work and talents turning him into a respected leader writer as well as drama critic.

Montague and Scott shared the same political views and between them they turned the Manchester Guardian into a vibrant and campaigning newspaper. Today it would be called a mission statement back then it was stated as "to bring all political action to the same tests as personal conduct".

This quickly led to their support of Irish Home Rule, a divisive issue at the time. Scott was now to take his views in front of the public and stand for Parliament. He was elected to serve between 1895 and 1906 and Montague now became the de facto editor of the paper. Once more the paper ran contrary to government policy and was in opposition to the Boer War which had begun to show many of the latent evils that war was to bring in terms of its brutalising conduct and the use of new technology and new ideas.

The relationship between Montague and Scott also became one of father and son-in-law when Montague married Scott's only daughter, Madeline, at the Unitarian Chapel in Manchester in 1898.

Montague had always had a great interest in literature and theatre and by the turn of the century was applauded as one of England's leading drama critics. Such was their insight and popularity that many of these essays were gathered together and later printed in book form.

As the storm clouds of war gathered over Europe in the summer of 1914 both Montague and Scott argued in the paper against Britain becoming involved in a war on the continent.

However argument was futile. When the Arch Duke was shot the dominos fell one after another. Britain intervened and went to the aid of its Allies. The First World War was now upon them with all its savagery and butchery.

Montague believed that it was important to give full and unequivocal support to the British government now that war was upon the Country. The general feeling that 'it will be all over by Christmas' became a realisation that it would drag on for years and the world now watched the horrific spectacle of trench warfare where tens of thousands were slaughtered for an advance of a few yards.

Montague wrote to Scott: "I have felt for some time, and especially since I have been writing leaders urging people to enlist, a strong wish to do the same myself. I wrote last week to the War Office to ask if there was any chance of getting over the difficulty of my few years over the limit of age, and I was told that although the War Office could not directly break the rule itself, it did not veto exceptions made by those responsible for the raising of new battalions locally."

Those 'few years' were, in fact, decades. Montague was now age forty-seven with a wife and seven children dependent upon him. Although his hair had been grey since his mid-twenties, he made a passable attempt at dying it darker in order to help persuade the army to take him. (or, as H. W. Nevinson put it in his witty and truthful way "Montague is the only man I know whose white hair in a single night turned dark through courage.") On 23rd December, 1914, the Royal Fusiliers accepted him and he joined the Sportsman's Battalion.

His military training was held at Climpson Camp in Nottingham. By November, 1915, Montague had been sent to France.

Upon his arrival on the Western Front, his commanding officer at once questioned the wisdom of having a man in his late forties in the trenches. Montague was sent before the Medical Board on 28th January 1916. He wrote "I went in and found the Colonel-Surgeon, who had barred me a month ago on the ground of my age, again presiding. He looked up at me genially, when I came to the table, and said, "So I hear you want to have another whack of the Germans". I admitted that I did. "How old are you - I mean, your real age?" "Forty-nine, Sir", said I, "but only just". "Sure you're fit?" I said yes. Another doctor at the table said something about my having been there before. "Yes, yes", said the Colonel, "I remember him perfectly. Well, Sergeant, all right", and he marked me a big 'A' on his report. I grinned and saluted and made off. He called after me as I was making for the door, "Sergeant, I believe you'll do better up there than some of the young uns".

Whatever the virtues of his patriotism it did help to bring about a new rule. Three months later it was announced that all men over forty four were to be banned from trench work.

Being a soldier in the trenches was hell on earth. You were either fighting, being shelled by artillery or living cheek by jowl in deep, muddy slits of earth where conditions can only best be described as appalling, the landscape often littered with dead and rotting corpses.

Montague wrote of the conditions to Francis Dodd: "The one thing of which no description given in England any true measure is the universal, ubiquitous muckiness of the whole front. One could hardly have imagined anybody as muddy as everybody is. The rats are pretty well unimaginable too, and, wherever you are, if you have any grub about you that they like, they eat straight through your clothes or haversack to get at it as soon as you are asleep. I had some crumbs of army biscuit in a little calico bag in a greatcoat pocket, and when I awoke they had eaten a big hole through the coat from outside and pulled the bag through it, as if they thought the bag would be useful to carry away the stuff in. But they don't actually try to eat live humans."

The journalist, Philip Gibbs, later recalled: "Prematurely white-haired, he had dyed it when the war began and had enlisted in the ranks. He became a sergeant and then was dragged out of his battalion, made a captain, and appointed as censor to our little group. Extremely courteous, abominably brave - he liked being under shell fire - and a ready smile in his very blue eyes, he seemed unguarded and open.

Once he told me that he had declared a kind of moratorium on Christian ethics during the war. It was impossible, he said, to reconcile war with the Christian ideal, but it was necessary to get on with its killing. One could get back to first principles afterwards, and resume one's ideals when the job had been done."

Montague was, as described earlier, a worker, a doer, and was soon promoted to the rank of second lieutenant and with it a transfer to Military Intelligence. For the next two years he had the task of writing propaganda for the British Army and censoring articles written by the five English journalists authorized to write, albeit with 'help' from the censor, on the Western Front.

Another of his duties was to escort important visitors for tours of the trenches. Among his charges were: David Lloyd George, Georges Clemenceau, George Bernard Shaw and H. G. Wells. (It is a bizarre thought now that this could happen but just over 60 years earlier many had picnicked with their wives on the hill-tops as the various battles of the Crimea war unfolded in the valleys below).

But the carnage also re-kindled his own feelings that War in the end solves little. Disillusioned by its scale, futility and bleak prognosis, he wrote a note in his diary in December 1917: "To take part in war cannot, I think, be squared with Christianity. So far the Quakers are right. But I am more sure of my duty of trying to win the war than I am that Christ was right in every part of all that he said, though no one has ever said so much that was right as he did. Therefore I will try, as far as my part goes, to win the war, not pretending meanwhile that I am obeying Christ, and after the war I will try harder than I did before to obey him in all the things in which I am sure he was right. Meanwhile may God give me credit for not seeking to be deceived."

George Bernard Shaw was one of those who Montague took for a tour of the frontline trenches: "At the chateau where the Army entertained the rather mixed lot who were classified as Distinguished Visitors, I met Montague. Finding him just the sort of man I like and get on with, I was glad to learn that he was to be my leader on my excursions. The standing joke about Montague was his craze for being under fire, and his tendency to lead the distinguished visitors, who did not necessarily share this taste into warm corners. Like most standing jokes it was inaccurate, but had something in it.... Both of us felt that, being there, we were wasting our time when we were not within range of the guns. We had come to the theatre to see the play, not to enjoy the intervals between the acts like fashionable people at the opera."

In November 1918 the war was over and Montague could now return home to his wife and family and also to the Manchester Guardian where he would continue to stay until retirement in 1925.

After the end of World War I Montague wrote in a strong anti-war vein; "War hath no fury like a non-combatant." Disenchantment (written in 1922), a collection of newspaper articles about the war, was one of the first prose works to strongly criticise the way the war was fought, and is a pivotal text in the development of literature about the First World War. Disenchantment criticised the British Press' coverage of the war and the conduct of the British generals. Montague accused the latter of being influenced by the "public school ethos" which he condemned as a "gallant robust contempt for "swats" and for all who invented new means to new ends and who trained and used their brains with a will".

Perhaps the paragraph in Disenchantment that most readily captures his overall feeling is: "The freedom of Europe, The war to end war, The overthrow of militarism, The cause of civilization - most people believe so little now in anything or anyone that they would find it hard to understand the simplicity and intensity of faith with which these phrases were once taken among our troops, or the certitude felt by hundreds of thousands of men who are now dead that if they were killed their monument would be a new Europe not soured or soiled with the hates and greeds of the old. So we had failed - had won the fight and lost the prize; the garland of war was withered before it was gained. The lost years, the broken youth, the dead friends, the women's overshadowed lives at home, the agony and bloody sweat - all had gone to darken the stains which most of us had thought to scour out of the world that our children would live in. Many men felt, and said to each other, that they had been fooled."

For Montague the war had been corrosive on his ideals, his faith and his time away from his young family. But it had given him much to write about both for the paper and also for his books which he now hoped to also spend more time working on. Among those to flow from his pen are the novels A Hind Let Loose and Rough Justice as well as collections of short stories, other essays and a travel book.

He finally retired in 1925, and settled down to become a full-time writer in the last years of his life.

C. E. Montague died in Manchester on May 28th, 1928 at the age of 61.

Today Montague is seen as an Edwardian writer who, in his best work, was able to deliver the reality of the situations with their corrosive emotions and doubts. Though undervalued, much of his work has now begun to be again recognised for its honesty and its literary value. A writer with a sharp eye and keen ear and a brain unafraid to think things through and give us the benefit of those thoughts.

His collected papers are archived at John Rylands University.

Montague also wrote some poetry. Much of the conflict between his Christian faith and his soldierly duties are summed up in this poem:-

Unnamed Lines

Yes, of course it was sin
And no Christ would say `Fight
For the right' -
But we had to win.

When the chaplain would bluster and blow
About laying the rod
Of God
On the back of `His foe',

I knew it was all just a form,
And there was no fiery sword,
And the Lord
Was not in the storm.

Yet - to have stood aside
Hoarding my fortunate life
With my wife
While other men died!

Some sort of god, good or bad,
Would have kept me longing in vain
To be slain
As I am, if I had.

Written sometime in 1917

C. E. Montague – A Concise Bibliography

Dramatic Values (1911) Reviews
The Morning's War (1913) Novel
Disenchantment (1922) Essays on the First World War]
Fiery Particles (1923) Short stories (Another Temple Gone/Honours Easy/My Friend the Swan/A propos des Bottes/The First Blood Sweep/In Hanging Garden Gully/All for Peace and Quiet/Two or Three Witnesses/A Trade Report Only
A Hind Let Loose (1924) Novel
The Right Place (1924) Travel writing
Rough Justice (1926) Novel
Right off the Map (1927) Science fiction novel
Action (1928) Short stories (Action/A Cock and Bull Story/Sleep, Gentle Sleep/Judith/In the Ways of his Heart/A Pretty Little Property/The Great Sculling Race/Wodjabet/A Fatalist/Man Afraid/Ted's Leave/The Wisdom of Mrs. Trevanna/Didn't take Care of Himself
A Writer's Notes on His Trade (1930)

www.ingramcontent.com/pod-product-compliance
Lightning Source LLC
Chambersburg PA
CBHW051305170626
46809CB00004B/1783